THE MURDER QUEENS 3

Michael Gallon

Lock Down Publications and Ca$h
Presents

The Murder Queens 3

A Novel by *Michael Gallon*

Michael Gallon
Lock Down Publications
Po Box 944
Stockbridge, Ga 30281

Visit our website @
www.lockdownpublications.com

Lock Down Publications
Like our page on Facebook: Lock Down Publications @
www.facebook.com/lockdownpublications.ldp
Book interior design by: **Shawn Walker**
Edited by: **Sunny Giovanni**

Stay Connected with Us!

Text **LOCKDOWN** to 22828 to stay up-to-date with new releases, sneak peaks, contests and more…

.

Thank you.

Submission Guideline.

Submit the first three chapters of your completed manuscript to ldpsubmissions@gmail.com, subject line: Your book's title. The manuscript must be in a .doc file and sent as an attachment. Document should be in Times New Roman, double spaced and in size 12 font. Also, provide your synopsis and full contact information. If sending multiple submissions, they must each be in a separate email.

Have a story but no way to send it electronically? You can still submit to LDP/Ca$h Presents. Send in the first three chapters, written or typed, of your completed manuscript to:

LDP: Submissions Dept
Po Box 944
Stockbridge, Ga 30281

DO NOT send original manuscript. Must be a duplicate.

Provide your synopsis and a cover letter containing your full contact information.

Thanks for considering LDP and Ca$h Presents.

DEDICATIONS

RIP to Earl, former manager of the club Hollywood Nites.

Michael Gallon

CHAPTER 1
A FAMILY BUSINESS

I fell back into my chair with my head in my hands as they all pulled up their clothing. "What in the hell is going on around here? You females are supposed to be a group of dancers, not hired professional killers. What and who's idea was this in the first place?"

Before they could even answer my question, I heard a familiar voice coming from my Television Room. "It was me, Baby Boy. Your sister Cynthia Vallentino!"

I jerked my head around to see my baby sister coming from out of the Television Room with a smile across her face. "What the hell, and how did you get in here?"

"It's nice to see you as well, baby brother!" she replied as she went to embrace me with a hug.

"Hold on, wait one minute. You're the baby of the family!" I said to her as we hugged one another as though we hadn't seen each other in years.

She causally smiled at me before leaning back and replying, "That might be so, but haven't I always been there for you whenever there was any sign of trouble coming your way."

I was about to open my mouth with her answer, when Mignon walked over and said, "Hey, Cynthia, we tried to keep this matter quiet and hush hush, but somehow word got about what we're doing."

The rest of the females greeted my sister with a hug as well.

"Have your identities been compromised in any way?" my sister asked as she greeted the ladies with a genuine smile.

"No, all we have heard is that it's a number of females going around killing for hire."

"Good. Y'all don't worry about Mike, I'll explain everything to him. You guys go ahead and enjoy yourself at the pool while my brother and I get reacquainted with one another."

The ladies all began to walk away when my damn brother walked in through the garage door, eating a big ass sub sandwich from Subway.

I was looking at him like *what the fuck*, then I recited, "Damn, thick-headed ass nigga. Didn't I tell you to wait at the hotel with Yani?"

"I know I was supposed to stay put with her at the hotel, but if I would have stayed there any longer, I would have fucked the shit out of that poor, beautiful, young girl!" he replied while grabbing the crotch of his brown Dickie shorts.

I was still astonished as I looked at the both of them and mumbled, "So, you and Cynthia, just done turned my lil' shit into a family business, I see."

CHAPTER 2
MORPHEOUS!

While Rhynyia lay there in her bed, fast asleep dreaming of the times when she and Michael were together, she didn't hear the door of her bedroom open, nor did she hear the gentlemen who softly tiptoed into her room, as she lay there in a comatose state with dreams of her Prince Charming dancing in her head. She hadn't realized that the group of brothers had entered into her room until her sensitive nose caught the familiar aroma that lingered throughout her bedroom.

At first, she thought that it was just an aroma she was smelling in her dreams, but just as quick as she had smelt the fragrance, she realized that she wasn't dreaming. *So,* the notion of it being in her dreams was quickly banished from her head. She then realized that there were intruders fast upon her as she eased her hand under her pillow, searching for her trusty Rugger nine millimeter. Once she had acquired her weapon, she thought of how many intruders were actually in her room, and if she had enough rounds to get off enough clean shots.

As soon as the first intruder was close enough for her to smell the familiar fragrance, Rhynyia sprung up from her bed with her weapon pointed directly at one of the intruders' head.

Meanwhile, back in Orlando, Florida, Cynthia had sat me down with my brother and explained her plan to me. I was somewhat baffled as to how she had convinced my closest females to become involved with the Murder Queens.

I had been going back and forth with her for about two hours when my brother stepped in and said to me, "Baby Boy, I know everything going on around you. must be a shock."

I looked back at him. "No, you think, Firstborn?" I replied sarcastically.

"Damn, that's how you feel?" he replied, while gulping down a cold can of Orange Crush soda.

"You're damn right, James! How would you feel if you just found out that some of your employees were doing more than just what they were supposed to be doing?"

He walked around to me, placing his arm on my shoulder. "Mike, believe me, I fully understand, but you have to see things from Cynthia's point of view."

While he was standing there trying to beat me over the head with the bullshit, my sister was standing up with her arms folded behind her back as if she were Morpheus in the movie The Matrix while looking out of the sliding glass door. She lethargically turned to look back at me and then mumbled, "Baby Boy, trust me when I tell you that you're going to need the protection that these girls have to offer."

I stood up facing her, walking into the kitchen, when I replied, "Guys, please, I understand that, but I don't need no extra heat over my head." I stood there watching the ladies swimming and splashing water on each other.

"I understand that. That's why we should offer those two crooked ass cops who keep harassing you a piece of the pie and then go from there," Cynthia said as she sat back down in one of my recliners that sat in the living room of the house.

"Now you and I both know how niggas can get once they see how much money that I'm bringing in. Hell, look at what had to be done about my old security guard," I said to the both of them as I started pacing back and forth in my living room.

"I feel you, Mike, but see your boy Bernard was just thirsty and wanted more than he could manage. Now, me, myself, I would've gave him like a hundred and fifty thousand to keep his fat mouth closed!" Cynthia voiced as she reclined back in the recliner that she was sitting in.

CHAPTER 3
SHIT JUST GOT REAL

I could sense the tension between the both of us as she sat there lounging in my chair. I then quickly came back at her with, "Yeah, okay, and then after he had spent all that up, he would have demanded more money. Ain't nobody have no damn time to keep paying his fat, nasty ass," I replied with a different tone in my voice.

My brother, who was still standing there between her and I chimed in with, "He's absolutely right about that, Cynthia. That big ass, trifling nigga would have been wanting a piece of the pie every other day of the week. And we all know that wasn't going to happen. So, we would've had to off him sooner or later anyway, with his fat, goat-smelling ass."

"Okay, I see your point, but I still feel like the Murder Queens can be a vital addition with the daily operation of what you have here, Baby Boy."

I sat there contemplating what she had just said. Then I took a good look at her and the girls and said, "Alright, Cynthia. I tell you what I'm going to do. Let me sleep on what we have discussed today, and I'll give you guys my answer by the end of the week."

"Alright. Mike, don't wait until it's too late and decide that we need them, when you should be making that decision right now. Hell, you just can't fire them, they know entirely too much. On top of that, them bitches are having too much fun doing what they're doing. Look how they all are acting out there at the pool; makes me want to get my ass out there and have some fun, too."

"She's right, Mike. If you let them go right now, they will be more of a problem than keeping them by your side," Firstborn said to me as he took the last gulp of his soda.

"Alright, so be it! But they're going to have to minimize all the damn killing. I mean it!"

"Mike, those girls are more than just your average day to day hired hit women. They all have their own individual unique way of taking out their adversaries. In other words, Baby Boy, them females right there are bad as hell when it comes to handling the steel." She then stood up and placed her hand on my shoulder and then whispered out loud, "This shit just got real for you and the Florida Hot Girls." An evil grin appeared on her face.

She was absolutely right, for I was about to find out, just as soon as we arrived in Tampa later that night.

CHAPTER 4
OFF THE BONE

Watching my sister pull out of my driveway in her brand new Snoop Dog Cadillac Sedan Deville made me smile to see her finally upgrade her vehicles of the past. As I watched her bend the corner of my street, headed out of the gate, I thought back to the time when she owned a silver lil' Dodge Colt Hatchback. I think it might have been her first car, and she loved that car with a passion.

It was one weekend that the both of us were driving back home from Madison, Florida. We had both been there for the weekend and on the way home she decided that she wanted to challenge me to a race. We were neck and neck coming down I-75 when I passed her by driving on the shoulder of the road. Once I was in the clear I jumped back in front of the following cars and pushed it.

Well, my lil' sister tried to do the same thing by passing some of the other cars while driving on the shoulder of the highway. Somehow, she got stuck in between some semi-tractor trailers who wouldn't let her merge back onto the highway in time for her to make the exit.

As I turned off the exit and waited for her at the truck stop, she never showed up. She told me after she got home hours later that she ended up all the way in Saint Petersburg. And the only way she got home was that she spotted a Church Van that had Lakeland, Florida on it, and followed them home.

While standing there laughing and reminiscing about the past I turned to walk back inside the house to find my brother outside by the pool kicking it with none other than everybody's girl, Strawberry, who he called *Scrawberry* because his country-talking ass couldn't pronounce the word *Strawberry*. I smiled at the sight of them, and then walked upstairs to my bedroom as Divia was walking out of the shower with nothing on but a towel that she was frantically using to dry herself off with.

I must admit she looked quite nice standing there butt ass naked with water glistening off of her beautiful body. I jumped in bed and placed my arms behind my head, still staring at her while she was drying her hair off, when she looked back at me and said to me with that country smile of hers, "Do you mind if I show your black ass how I eat the dick off of the bone?"

I smiled at her as I quickly responded with, "Not if you don't mind me putting your knees up by your ears."

She smiled at me as she answered, "Hell naw. I was hoping that you would put that long ass big black dick of yours all up in my stomach anyway."

CHAPTER 5
LARGE FOREHEAD

I was highly aroused as I laid there staring at the beautiful vixen. As usual my genuine smile beamed upon my gleeful face as I uttered, "Say no more, my stunning country bumpkin. Now get that saturated wet pussy of yours over here so that we can get down to the business at hand."

Thirty minutes later I thought that I was in a Pretty Ricky porn flick with the way I had her ass all twisted up while making love to her pretty ass. One minute she was on top of me and the next minute I was hitting her from the back, while knocking her head into the wall. We were making so hard and long that we had actually forgot that there were other people inside the house with us. That's when I heard Strawberry and my wild ass brother down the hall in her room, fucking as if they had been knowing each other for years.

Divia and I finished up an hour later, as she got up and went back for a second shower. While she went to the shower, I walked down to Strawberry's room naked, trying to spy on what my brother was putting her through.

I was shocked as I opened her door to see my brother with Strawberry in a compromising position. *What in the fuck?* No wonder Strawberry was hollering like she was. My brother was fucking her in the ass! "Nasty dick muthafucker," I said to myself while standing there watching the way he was drilling her poor lil' asshole. She was taking it in her ass as though she was a fucking porn star herself. Firstborn wasn't playing with her ass neither. It looked as if he had his whole entire arm sunk inside of her tight exit hole.

I was standing there in awe when Nicole walked up behind me and grabbed my manhood and started sucking me from the back. I looked down at her between my legs and mumbled, "Damn, I ain't never had my dick sucked like this before. I always wanted to see what this was like," as I smiled and thought about my boy Mike Epps when he said the same thing in the movie Friday. At first, I was startled then I fixed my mouth to say, "Nicole, wait a minute. What are you doing?"

My brother must've heard me as he turned his head and said, "Man, bring her lil' fine ass in here with us and fuck the shit out of her ass. Hell, that's all she's been talking about anyway!"

I still had the secretions from Divia all over my stiff manhood as she continued sucking on me, when she looked up at me and said, "Damn, Divia has some sweet ass pussy!"

"Why do you say that Nicole?" I asked her as she stood up, staring me directly in my eyes.

"Because I can taste her on this dick I'm sucking!"

By now my manhood had swollen up like a Ball Park Frank.

The both of us slowly walked into Strawberry's room.

When Strawberry turned her head around to witness us together, she voiced, "Damn, Mike, I didn't know that you were packing like that!"

"Yes, chick. Why do you think his ass be having these lil' bitches in here foaming for this dick. But you might as well get off his dick because you can't have any!" Nicole replied to Strawberry as she began slurping on my manhood once again.

"Oh, so you looking at my brother's dick while I'm up inside of your ass? I tell you what, I'm about to knock the bottom out of your ass for disrespecting me like that!" Firstborn said to Strawberry with veins popping out of his quite large forehead.

CHAPTER 6
THE CALL

We were all inside that room with it partly smelling like ass and feet when Strawberry took my brother's dick out of her ass and then shoved into her mouth without wiping it off at all. She had his manhood by the base as she looked up at my brother and muttered, "Let me show you how I eat the dick off of the bone!" Her eyes began to enlarge as my brother started ramming his manhood down her throat.

Nicole was just as stunned as I was when she said, "With the way he is jamming his dick down her throat, she's going to eat the shit off of his dick before he hits the back of her poor lil' mouth." We all burst into laughter and kept right on going hard, for I had to hurry up and get mine before Divia started looking throughout the house for me.

Twenty minutes later, Nicole had just finished catching her second orgasm, so it was just a matter of time before I caught mine.

Meanwhile it wasn't until thirty minutes later when Firstborn was cumming all up inside of Strawberry who was just lying there on the bed, smiling at this crazy looking ass nigga, who resembled the Incredible Hulk in the face, with all the ugly ass facial expressions he was making during the course of knocking her head off.

While watching all this take place, I couldn't help but ask myself, "Damn, Strawberry has slept with my cousin the whole entire weekend, now she's here sleeping with my brother. I sure hope that Richard didn't develop any serious feelings for her over the weekend. If so, he was about to have some intense problems on his hands."

My foolish ass brother had just fucked the poor girls brains out! I didn't think that nobody else would be able to have sex with her for at least a week or two, especially with the way she was laying there fanning her pussy. I was trying not to laugh at the way she looked with a fat ass frown covering her face.

Within minutes I had finally burst inside of Nicole. After she wiped us off, I was busy walking back to my room when she yelled out to me from the hallway, "I want some more later, Michael!"

I looked back at her and put my index finger up to my lips. "Shh, okay, Nicole. Once Divia leaves, you're gonna get a whole lot more. Just be patient, my dear."

She smiled at me and then turned to walk back to her room.

By the time I got back to my room, Divia was laying there in bed fast asleep. *Good. Now I can take a quick shower and try to enjoy the rest of the day before we have to head out to the club.*

When I finished taking a long hot shower it was then that I noticed that I had ten missed calls. I stood there dripping wet as I thumbed through all the missed calls, trying my best not to wake Divia, when I happened to notice a peculiar number staring back at me. I stood motionless while pondering the notion of calling the number back for a brief minute or so, but after a few minutes of deliberating I decided to make the call, not knowing who would answer on the other end.

CHAPTER 7
PRINCE NAHEED!

The stunned men stood still, shitless, as they came face to face with the deadly Puerto Rican Princess who held the weapon firmly in her hand. Once their eyes met, Rhynyia screamed out, "Father, what are you and my uncles doing walking up on me like that? Don't you realize that you all could've been killed?"

Her father immediately placed his right hand into his chest and replied, "My dear, we meant not to frighten you. Please forgive me and my brothers. Welcome home!"

"I should've known that it was you when I smelled your cologne," Rhynyia voiced as she sprang out of bed to embrace her father and uncles.

An elegant smile beamed over her face as she placed her arms around the neck of her father, Pierre Santiago, who she hadn't seen in years. It was the same reaction as she hugged her uncles' individual necks and greeted them all with a smile, since it had been ages since she'd seen all of them together at the same time.

She hadn't seen her father since her 18th birthday. Now that she was twenty-five years old, it was hard to believe that it had been seven years too long since she had seen him last.

He still had the chiseled body that he adorned from many years of working out and staying fit. Her dear father always made sure that he kept his appearance and body in the best of shape. Even though he loved Rhynyia's stepmother, he was still some type of man-whore in their small, heavily populated country. One thing for certain was that he made sure he kept his extra marital activities at bay so that it wouldn't interfere with his cherished family life. In other words, he was a dog, but he was still her father, who she loved very much.

"Good morning to you, father. When did you get in?" A radiant looking Rhynyia asked as she began searching the room for her belongings, so that she could prepare herself for the rest of the family.

"A few hours ago, my young, beautiful princess."

"How was your trip back home, father?"

"My journey back here was fine the constant thought of seeing your beautiful face is what kept me looking forward to being here," he said to her as he smiled with every word that came out of his mouth.

"So where did you come from?" she asked.

"That's not what's important right now, princess. What I need now is for you to get dressed so that we all can enjoy breakfast together as a family," he recited as he held out his arms for her to hug him once again.

"Yes, father, give me a few minutes so that I can get myself together."

"Take your time, young lady. We're not going any-where anytime soon," her uncle Lorenzo replied as they all walked out of her room.

While her father and his brothers walked out of her room, Rhynyia stood there realizing that a major portion of her immediate family was all present under one roof at the same exact time. Her uncle Lorenzo, who was born right after her father. Then there was her uncle Hector, and then finally the baby boy, her dear uncle Felix. As she stood there in the mirror washing her face, she mumbled to herself, "It must be time for the family to put together a plan of attack for the ill-timed death of my brother, Prince Naheed."

CHAPTER 8
THE OLD MAN

After she had finished up at the bathroom sink, she was busy inside one of her bags of many things to choose from. While looking through her items she stood back and looked at herself in the full-length mirror.

"My God, I can see my lil' baby bump already. I must be at least a few weeks pregnant," she said to herself after seeing the small lump in her belly. Then she noticed the size of her face in the mirror. She knew then that it was probably best if she let her father know about the baby, that she and I were expecting.

Moments later there was a small knock at the door, that somewhat startled her. "One minute please," she shouted back behind the door.

"Rhynyia, it's me, Maylia," her youngest sibling yelled back from the other side of the bedroom door.

"Damn, I sure as hell can't let her in here and see me like this. Where are my t-shirts? Oh, here they are," she said to herself as she quickly placed on one of her Florida Hot Girl t-shirts. She then opened the door to a wide eye young girl, as she muttered, "Good morning, Maylia."

"Good morning to you, Rhynyia. Are you joining us for breakfast?"

"Yes, Maylia, I was just trying to get dressed when you burst into my room," Rhynyia said to her sister as the young lad flopped down on Rhynyia's bed.

"I can't believe that all of our uncles are here with us!" Maylia expressed with joy and excitement.

"Yes, that caught me by surprise also, Maylia! I guess that they are here to discuss the burial of Naheed," she said as she sat down next to her younger sister.

The younger version of Rhynyia looked up at her sister with a dreary face and replied, "Yes, maybe. They never tell me anything around here since I'm the youngest daughter."

Rhynyia had stood up, walking towards the mirror when she turned around and asked her sister, "How did he die, Maylia? I only received a brief description of what took place."

"Like I told you, Rhynyia, no one has really talked about how and why it happened. We all moved here right after it happened for the family's safety. Then father called his contact over in the States. The next thing we knew was that you were on father's private jet headed back here."

Their nosey ass grandfather poked his short grey-haired head inside the room. He was barely able to stand due to his declining health. Rhynyia saw him standing there at the door with his cane barely being able to hold him up when he called out to her. "My dearest grandchild, I see that you have returned home!"

She quickly darted to his side so that she could keep him from falling down as she hugged his neck and then placed him down in one of the chairs that sat adjacent to her bed.

"Thank you, my dear," he said as the wind from his lungs barely escaped his slow beating chest.

"Oh, papa, it's so nice to see you up and walking around. When I arrived, they told me that. You were ill and in bed," Rhynyia said as she sat down at his feet.

"Barely, my dear. Once I was told that all of my dear sons were here with my very first grandchild, I had to get to my feet so that I couldn't be forgotten," he said as he coughed heavily in between his slurred sentences.

"Papa, how could we forget about you? Because of you, all this was made possible," Rhynyia said as she looked up at the eyes of her aging grandfather.

CHAPTER 9
EATING FOR TWO!

The old man angrily coughed up some greenish looking phlegm as he tried to continue talking with Rhynyia and Maylia.

"Oh dear papa. Let me get you something to wash your hands with." Rhynyia yelped as she darted to the bathroom. She hurriedly came back with a wash towel as she helped him wipe himself clean of the awful looking phlegm.

He lethargically looked into her eyes and then spoke. "I would agree with you, but the lifestyle that you children have grown to love is all due to your father and his brothers acquiring the family business and turning it into a Global Empire."

Maylia and Rhynyia sat there attentively listening to the words coming from his mouth, of how the family came from nothing into being the wealthiest family in Puerto Rico.

"Papa, I still can't believe that Naheed is gone," Rhynyia said as she lowered her head.

"There is no need to be full of sorrow and grief, my dear. Now that you're here, things shall be fine," he replied as he kissed her on her forehead. He then mumbled, "Now hurry up and get yourself dressed. We have so much to talk about."

"Yes, papa, I shall be there in about ten minutes."

He then looked over at Maylia and beckoned for her to help him downstairs.

As they both walked out of her room, she was able to finish getting ready so that she could join the family for breakfast. It was around 9:15AM and she was still a tad bit tired, but she had just enough energy to pull herself together so that she could join the family. Once downstairs, she felt good to be amongst family once again. She just longed for her brother to be by her side.

Her father sat at the head of the table as it was family tradition for the head of the family to sit at the head of any table the family sat around. Her beautiful stepmother adorned his right side. With her uncle Lorenzo at the left of him; the rest of the family sat in their respectful places.

Just as Rhynyia went to take her seat, her father motioned for her to come and sit next to him. He then instructed her stepmother to sit in the chair that she was about to sit in. For some strange reason he wanted Rhynyia next to him, as he leaned over and whispered into her ear, "It has been too long since I saw you last. My dear wife will understand why I want you to sit next to me." He looked back at everyone sitting before them.

The table was laid with everything one could imagine when it came to eating breakfast. From the pork bacon to the country sausage, the Belgian waffles to the French toast and hot butter milk pancakes. Scrambled eggs to even eggs to order. Topped off with grits and hash browns.

The family all held hands as her grandfather blessed the food that they were about to consume. Once he finished, they all greeted one another and then started passing the food around. The family never talked business at the table where they ate their meals. So, everyone spoke of happier times until Countess, her second sister said something out of character.

"So, Nyia, how is your boyfriend doing back in Orlando, Florida? It is Orlando right?"

Rhynyia was caught off guard as she lifted up her head and replied, "He's fine. Why do you ask?"

She cleared her throat and then replied, "Because since you've been home I haven't heard you speak of this man."

"I think of him every day. Each day that I'm away from him is one more day that I miss him even more. But to think of him causes me to become lonely in my heart and mind," Rhynyia said to her sister as she tried to force a piece of bacon down her throat knowing that she was eating for two, so she had to make herself ingest the bacon and a few other items that were prepared for them.

Michael Gallon

CHAPTER 10
WITH THE FAMILY

Countess looked back over at Rhynyia with a devious smirk on her face and asked, "So, you become lonely even around family?"

By now Rhynyia was becoming a bit perturbed with her sister, and sarcastically replied, "Yes, Countess, this man that I'm in love with means the world to me!"

Her uncle Lorenzo sipped on his third cup of coffee. He slowly sat the cup down and chimed in. "Well, if this man means so much to you, why didn't you bring him here with you?"

The entire family sat there, waiting on her response.

Rhynyia then cleared her throat and said, "When I got the call that I had to return back home, I was told to just bring a few things and myself."

"Well, Princess, if by having this man you call Michael here by your side during a crucial time like this, I see no reason why he shouldn't be here amongst family," her uncle Lorenzo said while looking around at everyone sitting at the table.

Rhynyia looked to her father and then asked, "So, is it okay with you, father, if he comes here to visit and be my side at the funeral?"

Her father looked back at Rhynyia while placing down his glass of orange juice. His face held a broad smile as he muttered, "If this is what makes you happy I would certainly agree with my brother, for you to have this man here with you and the family."

Countess was smiling harder than Rhynyia as she uttered, "So, we're finally going to meet your boyfriend, Nyia!"

"I guess so, Countess," Rhynyia replied, eating her breakfast, and smiling as well at the thought of me being by her side. She couldn't wait until she called me, to let me know the good news. She would have me there with her family as they all prepared for the burial of her brother.

As she sat there looking at each one of her family members, she could feel the cold stare of someone at the table. As she finished the portion of her breakfast, she looked up to witness the cold stare coming from her oldest sister Natasha. At first Rhynyia cut a smile at her and nodded her head at her, waiting on her acknowledgement.

Her sister in turn just politely smiled back at her and turned her head towards their father. The entire time that they all sat at the table and had breakfast it seemed as if her oldest sister felt some type of way against her, ever since Rhynyia had been back home.

Rhynyia figured she would address the issue later after breakfast. What was on her mind now was that her father had no problems with me being there with her. She knew her father was a very sneaky man and if he didn't mind a total stranger being there, he must have had another reason why he wanted me over there with her. Rhynyia knew she would have to warn me about doing any business with her father or his brothers, due it being the death of many men who either failed or double-crossed them in any kind of way. A mistake that she couldn't let her future baby's father fall into.

She had just excused herself from the table when she decided to give me a call. We must have been thinking of each other at the same time. While she was about to dial my number, I was already calling her.

The phone rung one time as she answered. "Hey, Michael, what's up? I was just about to call you and tell you the good news!" she said sounding all excited.

"Nothing much, baby girl, just sitting here thinking about you. What's good?" I replied.

"Whatever, Michael, you probably just got through fucking!"

Damn, how did she know? Did she have cameras in here

or something? I said to myself while she started rambling a mile a minute on the other end of the phone.

Michael Gallon

CHAPTER 11
MY FAMILIES DRUG EMPIRE!

I quickly answered back, hoping that she couldn't detect the truth. "Nyia, for real. C'mon, girl. I wouldn't dare cheat on you while you're away grieving over your dear brother."

"Yeah, you better not, because if I find out I would hate to have to explain to our newborn child how I had to kill their father!" She meant that.

"Damn, Rhynyia, that's how you feel?" I asked with a whimper in my voice.

"For sho, my nigga."

"Well, we ain't gonna have to worry about that, because I'm not going to try you like that," I said as I crept out of the bedroom where Divia was lying there fast asleep.

"Okay, that's what I'm talking about," she voiced.

"So, what's up? How is it down there in Puerto Rico?" I asked trying to change the conversation.

"Everything is fine, Michael, and I'm not in Puerto Rico. I'm on a small island outside of Puerto Rico. The reason I was trying to call you was to inform you that my family says that since I'm so lonely here without you that I should have you down here with me a for a little while."

"That's what's up. I would love to come down there for a little while. That would be a nice vacation for me!" I replied with sheer excitement, due to me never being in Puerto Rico.

"But, Michael, I have to warn you about something," Rhynyia replied with a bit of procrastination in her voice.

"What's that, Rhynyia?" I asked with a slight bit of skepticism running through my mind.

"My father!" she replied, as I stood there wondering what she meant by her father.

"What about your father, Rhynyia?"

"Michael, I think that he wants to somehow incorporate

you into his business scheme," she replied with a side of mass concern in her voice.

"Aw, Nyia, that's it? Don't worry. Your father will be alright. I'm not that easily influenced," I replied as I smiled back into the phone.

"No, Michael, you don't understand. My father is a very perplexing man, and did I mention dangerous and very powerful? Significantly powerful! I think that he wants you to somehow smuggle some of the family's drugs back into Miami."

"Nyia, what makes you think something like that?"

"Because he's the type of guy that only deals with someone if they can be some type of assistance to him and his illegal drug trade empire. I'm not sure yet, but I believe that is what caused my brother Naheed his untimely death."

I was astonished for a brief minute when I came back with, "Well, when it comes to drugs, Rhynyia, you know that's one thing that I don't deal with!"

"Well, all I know is that when you get here, please, Michael, I beg of you to stay away from his drugs, please!" she said to me with a sign of apprehension in her voice.

"Rhynyia, I promise you sweetheart, I will not partake in any business deals with your father. Now when is the funeral?"

"Some time in the next few days."

"Will it be this week?"

"No, silly, the following week."

We continued to speak with one another for about another thirty minutes before we hung up. She had told me that she would call me back later to let me know the day and time that her father's private jet would be sent to pick me up.

CHAPTER 12
THAT'S FOR DAMN SHO!

Sunday night, it was like 8:30, and the girls at the house were all busy getting dressed for the club. I was still a bit tired from all of the love making and stressful events that I had been going through all day. Mignon was busy making sure the girls would be ready in time, while Nicole was on the phone calling the other ladies to let them know that we would be on our way to pick them up, shortly.

When we finally got to Apollo South, the club was packed to capacity as the patrons waited for the arrival of the world-famous Florida Hot Girls. Tonight, Richard and his crew of girls, along with the girls I had called team A, would be in full effect.

I was standing over by the dressing room while all the ladies got dressed when this short light skinned brother from St. Pete approached me with this lame ass story about him and his homies having a game room over on Fourth Street. Now I really wasn't too familiar with St. Pete and I really didn't want to go back over there since the last time that I had to go over there was to pick up Innocence who was no longer with the group.

"Man, when I tell you it's a real nice spot and you and your girls will definitely make some money. It will be a whole lot better than your females going over to Lou Doc's and making no money at all," he said to me as I saw the desperation written all over his face, for some bad ass exotic dancers.

"Okay, I tell you what. Let me talk it over with my cousin and I'll let you know something before the club closes."

"Sounds like a plan, my man. And to show you that I'm serious, here is five hundred dollars up front. And if you decide not to come, just keep the bread."

I looked down on the short brother and quickly replied, "Damn, bro, since it's like that. I tell you what. We will come, but please understand this, my girls are not doing any fucking for money!"

"Mike, that's cool with me. My guys and I understand that you're not a pimp. So, we respect that, my brother. We just want your bad ass females to grace our spot so that we can throw some dollars at their fine assess."

"Cool, so that we have an understanding. We will follow you guys over to your spot once the club closes."

"Thanks, see you in a few." He walked away smiling at the anticipation of seeing my girls over at his place later, when JK walked up on me from the dressing room.

"Mike, what do we have planned after the club?" she asked in that squeaky ass voice of hers.

"Well, JK, that guy who just walked away from me wanted me to bring you all over to his spot after the club so that you guys can make some extra cash."

"Sounds good to me, Mike, because we definitely don't want to go to no damn Lou Doc's after we leave here!" she replied while standing in front of me with her camel toe staring directly back at Johnboy, as if she wanted to test him out.

I looked back at her lovely smile and camel toe and then recited, "Oh, even if we didn't have anything to do we wasn't going back over there, that's for damn show!"

CHAPTER 13
YEAH RIGHT

Just as JK was about to walk away, I briskly grabbed her by her arm and said, "I know it's still early and we just got to the club and all but have all the girls to dress back in around one forty five, so that we can get out of here without getting held up."

"Yes, Mike." She walked away swaying her nice hips from side to side.

"Damn, she has a fat, stupid ass!" I shouted as my cousin stood beside me smiling at her nice ass cheeks.

He looked at me at me and then asked me, "So, Mike, is it like this every night?"

I looked back at his young eager smiling ass. "Aw, Richard, my dear boy, it's like this wherever I bring the girls to dance at. Now just kick back and enjoy yourself and make sure you collect your money, lil' young ass nigga!"

And that's exactly what he did, just sat back and collected his money, with neither one of us knowing what was about to take place at the next party that we all were headed to.

Two hours later we were sitting back at our table chilling and kicking back when he leaned over to me and said, "Hey cousin, let me ask you something?"

"Yeah Rich, what's on your mind now?"

"How do you maintain all these chicks and you don't fuck any of them?"

I looked back at him and said, "What are you saying Richard? I sleep around with a few of them. I just make sure that we keep it on the down low. You see the key to having dancers is that if you start fucking them, they're not going to want to pay your black ass at the end of the night. So, you got to get with just one and make her your special someone, and then follow that rule to the T and you will go a very long way in this business. The most important rule of all is don't fall in love with your main bitch, because it's *going* to hurt you deep in the end when she decides to leave you for a few more dollars that the next nigga has to offer her trifling ass!"

He just sat there taking in what I had just said, when he looked back over at me. "Damn, that's some serious fucking shit you just said partner!"

"Oh and by the way, don't let the next female know that you have fucked the next female, or you will get your feelings hurt for real when it comes to trying to collect your money at the end of the night!"

Rich sat there listening to me with his mouth wide the fuck open as I tried to explain the rules to his ass. He really didn't pay to close attention to what I was saying, for he would end up getting fired a few months later for not following that valuable advice. I should've fired him that same night for letting what happened next happen to me at all!

By 1:30 the club was dying down and it looked like we would be leaving early.

The guy from St. Pete came by my table again just to make sure that everything was still a go. He was at the table with all smiles as he looked at Richard and I and said to the both of us, "I called my partners, and everything is on point. My boy says that everything is set up and ready for your arrival."

"Sounds like a plan to me, lil' ass nigga. I'm gonna have my girls go ahead and get dressed back in and we'll be ready to head out with you."

We embraced each other with a quick handshake and went from there, with me thinking that everything was cool as cool could be. Yeah right!

CHAPTER 14
ALWAYS ABOUT THAT PAPER

As I sat there listening to the words coming from the guy's mouth, I could hear my sister in the back of my mind telling me how much I needed the Murder Queens. She would be right in the end, due to me needing them sooner than I thought.

Just as the guy walked away from the table, I looked over at Richard and said, "Hey Rich, let your girls know that it's about that time and also tell them that we're about to head to another club. Hey, and tell them females that I'm not having that VIP shit tonight, we about to make this paper and then get the fuck out of St. Pete!"

He looked back at me smiling and just happy to be a part of what I had started. "I gotcha, cousin. I'm 'bout to round up my crew right now," he said to me as he walked his lil' shy ass away headed for the girls dressing room.

By now it was around 1:45 and it was still a few guys throwing some money at some of the ladies. I motioned for Divia so that she could get her bags and have the rest of the girls follow her to the vehicle.

When I walked by the dance floor I spotted this one lil' slim dark chick still on the floor snatching up dollars, acting like she was busy getting money. She saw me and the girls walking by the stage area and then started yelling to the rest of the girls, "Hey, don't y'all fucking leave me! I'm trying to get this money for my rent!"

I walked outside behind the girls to see everyone else at the different vehicles putting their bags inside, while some of the guys from the club were outside the truck trying to get their individual phone numbers. I was staring down the ones who knew better than to try one of my rules and give out their phone number, when I heard Nicole tell Mignon, "Now them chicks know damn well that Mike don't play about them giving out their phone numbers!"

"Yep, they'll either be fired by tomorrow or have a fat ass fine to pay!" Mignon barked as she turned her head to see who all were inside of the truck ready to leave.

"Okay is everyone in here?" I asked as I started my truck.

"No, Mike, that one lil' black ass chick is still inside the club dancing!" Lil' Kitty screamed while smiling at everyone as usual.

"Well she must be staying down here in Tampa tonight, because we have another show to get to over in St. Pete!" I shouted back at the females.

"I'll go get her black ass, Mike!" Entyce shouted as she jumped out of the truck, running back inside the club. She had just go to the entrance of the club, when she shouted to the young female, "Yo, Michelle, Mike is about to leave your skinny black ass here! Are you coming or what?"

She speedily picked up her few ones off of the dance floor and ran behind Entyce, half naked, trying to get inside the truck before she got left. After I gave her ass a real good cussing out, she said to me, almost about to cry, "Mike, I was just trying to make my money because my rent is due tomorrow!"

I was already headed down 40th Street when Charlie B turned to look at her sitting in the backseat of the truck with tears welling up in the bottom of her eyes. "Girl, we're headed to St. Pete right now to some after-hour spot so that we can make some more cash!"

Michelle started bouncing up and down, screaming as I merged onto interstate 275, "That's what the fuck I'm talking about! That's why I'm in this fucking group! Mike always be about his muthafucking paper!"

CHAPTER 15
SWEETNESS!

The entire truckload of beautiful women all burst out with laughter when they heard Michelle's quick-witted remark. Not to mention myself, while following the guy to his spot over in St. Pete.

Richard and his crew of females followed close behind as we all looked forward to making a nice sizeable amount of money at the next stop.

That night I had a few more new chicks with us, one of them was from the small town where I picked up Strawberry, known to all by the name of Haines City. Pecan-tan looking female who went by the name of Linda— she stood around five foot seven and probably weighed a hundred and thirty-five pounds. She had nice small perky lil' tits to go along with the nice proportioned body she adorned. I would find out later on a trip to Miami that Linda had something else that she held on her body. Something so sinister that it would prevent her from ever dancing inside Club Coca's, one of Miami's finest strip clubs. Then there were the three new chicks from Orlando. Now what I liked about them was the fact that they were all fine and quite serious about getting to the money.

First it was the one chick named Coca, who stood around five foot six and weighed a hundred and forty pounds with a thirty-six D size bra. Her skin complexion was just a tad bit dark brown, but it would suffice. Then it was the one named Peaches. Peaches stood around the same height as Coca, with some nice size titties that always seemed to protrude out of whatever she wore to cover up those beautiful twins that she carried on her chest. Her ass was nice and tight, which made her fit right in with the crew of lovely ladies on my team. Last but not least was their special friend, who called herself Sweetness. Now

Sweetness was the picture-perfect female, just like I liked them. Red bone who weighed around a hundred and twenty-five pounds. She stood a mere five foot four and had the nicest ass that I had ever seen.

At first sight of this Nubian Princess, I wanted what all men wanted when laying eyes on her beauty. But she wasn't having it. Telling me that she didn't want to mix business with pleasure. Something I would have to remember, especially when it came to collecting my money. Sweetness was so attractive and elegant that she kind of reminded me of a younger version of my darling Sexy Redd. At first sight I thought about making her Sexy Redd's replacement. But as it may, that notion would drastically be changed by the end of that morning, due to a stunt that only she could pull and get away with.

Like I said, shit was about to get muthafucking real for the Florida Hot Girls and myself. If only I would've listened to my sister when it came to having them females by my side, known as the infamous Murder Queens.

CHAPTER 16
SMELLING HER ASS

We finally arrived in St. Pete, with the ladies all being hyped up about dancing at a new spot, one in which they could call their very own, All while being able to collect some extra cash while establishing the new spot as theirs. We would soon— or should I say I was soon— to find out that we were all very wrong.

As we all walked into the nice size building that they had as their local town game room, the DJ had the spot jumping with the song *Lights, Cameras, Action*, the remix version by Mr. Cheeks and Pete Pablo. The ladies heard the song blaring through the sound system and began swaying from side to side, while throwing their hands up in the air and singing right along with the song.

I had my head bobbing along with the music as well, as I searched throughout the club for where my ladies were going to dress in.

While standing there looking around, Strawberry walked up to me with, "I guess I won't be fucking anything up in here this morning, huh, Mike?"

I stared back at her intensively and replied, "I know damn well that you won't, because I ain't having that VIP shit going on here!" I recited it with a very icy, cold, stale look on my face.

She then looked back at me and mumbled, "Nah, your wild ass brother beat the brakes off of my lil' twang-twang. It hurts just by looking at it," she replied with a half-smile on her face.

"Damnnnn, my brother hit that thang like that?" I asked her with a devilish smirk on my face.

"Yep. And besides, Richard said that he wants me to relax and just take it easy."

"So let me get this straight, Strawberry. You're going to

play my brother and my cousin at the same damn time?"

She looked at me with a very serious unit on her face and then uttered, "Mike, I wasn't playing with you when I told you that I wanted to be in your family!"

"Well, you sure as hell ain't going to get in the family by fucking my brother and my retarded ass cousin, ole silly ass girl!"

She just smiled at me and walked away trying to find out where the rest of the ladies were so she could get dressed for the show.

By now all the ladies had dressed and I was waiting for the first one of them to come out so they could all follow behind one another. I looked over at a few of them as they strutted out of the dressing room, admiring all the nice expensive cars in the parking lot, when I shouted out to them. "If y'all know like I do, that doesn't mean a damn thing! It's what's in them niggas' pockets that count!"

They were all looking around for someone to dance on when Lil' Redd just took off and went to the first guy she saw who looked like he might have some money inside of his pockets. Once she started shaking her lil' nice red ass I thought about hitting her lil' nice ass again. I was standing there debating the thought and then said to myself that I couldn't keep mixing her emotions up with what she was trying to do. So I would have to just wait until later to once again give her the sexual experience of her young life.

I then turned away from gazing at her dancing on her first customer, when Suga Bear pulled me by my arm and uttered, "It's a lot of nice cars outside in the parking lot isn't it?"

"Yeah, I guess. Hell, half of you girls could be driving the same kind of cars, if y'all would just save your money instead of spending it as soon as you make it!"

She just rolled her lil' beady eyes back at me and walked away with her nice round ass swaying from side to side, with Peekachu walking right behind her as if she was smelling Suga Bear's ass.

Michael Gallon

CHAPTER 17
WAITING TO BE KILLED

By now, all of my top-notch females were making damn good money for being considered strippers. For example, JK was bringing in somewhere in the neighborhood of $4,000 a week, while her friend from Ocala named Bridget was bringing in a stunning $3,000 a week. Her next female in charge was Kizzy. Kizzy was somewhere in the range of $1,5000 whenever she wasn't stealing stuff off of the internet. Since Charlie B had been back in the group, she was commanding at least $2,500 a week. While your girl Lil' Kitty was making so much fucking money, that if the IRS would have found out, she would have been in someone's jail for tax invasion. That's Just how much money she was bringing in every week. I would always tease her about the amount of cash she was making, but for some strange reason she claimed that she didn't know where all of her money went. She would realize some twelve years later that the local weed man that she was going to had made so much money off of her lil' narrow ass that he eventually retired from the dope game, all thanks to Lil' Kitty.

Nicole and Ms. Tight Coochie both had fat ass bank accounts, as well, since the both of them said that they were saving up for a rainy day. Meanwhile, Peekachu and Suga Bear were both just balling with their new life of wealth, fortune, and fame. Now when it came to the both of them saving any of their hard-earned cash, they would always tell me, "We can always make more money at the next show, so why keep it?"

Mignon was making so much money that she kept her amount to herself. Your girl Lovely was making mad money also and whatever she wasn't making in the club, she claimed that Superstar Rated R was paying her the rest. She was going around bragging that Rated R had put her in one of his songs. I think it was the hit record called *In Here*

Tonite. Now I have listened to that song a million times and still haven't heard her name in that damn song.

The ladies had been dancing at the lil' Trap Spot in St. Pete for at least two hours or so. I was busy looking for Richard's block headed ass while the DJ had the spot jumping to *In Here Tonite* when Lovely jumped her big black happy ass on one of the pool tables screaming, "That's the song that Rated R said that he made especially for me!" she screamed as she began shaking that big black ass of hers.

I looked over at her and yelled back, "Yeah right, Lovely! Get your ass down before you fall and break your crazy ass neck or something!"

The girls were all yelling and screaming for me to change in their ones, as a few of them kept right on dancing along with the song. While all of that was going on, I kept feeling like someone or something was watching me throughout the morning. I should've brought my brother with me that night, but his ass was too damn tried to get out of bed after fucking Strawberry all day.

After that night I would regret ever doubting my sister when it came to those girls called the Murder Queens.

Something was about to go down in that club and I would be caught right there in the muthafucking middle, without any protection nor any heat on my waist. In other words, I was a duck in open waters, while sitting there waiting to be killed.

CHAPTER 18
THESE YOUR BITCHES?

I continued to sit there and keep an eye on my girls with no one there to keep an eye on me. At least that's what I thought.

While Richard was still over in the corner sipping on something brown in his cup and playing pool with his good smoking partner Chazz, I casually walked over to the both of them while he was holding his pool stick in his hand.

He looked up at me and said, "Cuz, you play?"

"Why of course, Richard. I play a lil' something. I'm not as good as our cousin Eddie Junior but I can handle my own with the stick." So while he was racking up the balls, I asked him. "Damn, cousin, I didn't know that you smoke weed or even drank."

"Hell, Mike, doing this type of work and being around all of this pussy and ass, I had to start doing something or else lose my mind around all these bad ass females," he said to me while having the blunt barely hanging from his mouth.

All I could say to him was, "Well, don't get to fucked up. You're still at work and have a serious job to do!"

"And what's that, cousin? I thought that all I had to do was just count this money and babysit these females."

"Yes, that's part of the job description, but you forgot one of the most important components of the job!"

"Really, what's that?" he asked with a quizzical look on his face.

Before I could reply with an answer, Chazz came over and snatched the blunt that he was smoking right out of his mouth. Without wiping it off, she placed it right dab smack off in her small ass mouth. Ewww, she didn't even wipe it off. She just placed up in her mouth as though it was a dick and started pulling on it, while Richards block headed ass just kept right on talking and trying to shoot pool.

"The answer to your question my boy, is always making sure that you have my back covered at all times, playa!"

He stood up after missing his shot and replied, "Cuz, no need to worry. I'm always watching your back!"

Now that was a lot that I was asking him to do, since I was the one who killed his kids' mother. And now here I was asking him to watch my back. What a fucked-up way to look at it. But that's life and the way that some things in life are meant to be.

Now after I had beat him three games to none and after about two or three hours, the spot was really jumping, and the females were both throwing money at each other, just having a good ole time. The DJ still had the spot jumping with *Forget Tha Otha Side* by the Dunk Ryders. A few of the girls were on top of the pool tables dancing and kissing one another in the mouth. Just doing about anything they could to draw some attention their way, so they could continue to get their money.

I was busy making change for the ones who were throwing money. It was so many girls there that I really couldn't watch all of them to make sure they were alright.

While walking around one of the guys who I guessed was part owner of the lil' night spot approached me with, "Hey, you the nigga that's in charge of all these bitches?" He asked me with a lil' base in his voice.

I looked him up and down and then voiced, "Hold on homie, why do they have to be called bitches?"

CHAPTER 19
SHIT EVER WENT DOWN

We were both eye to eye as the young man replied, "'Cause that's what these hoes are, a bunch of low-class bitches!" He replied as if he was challenging me to a fist fight.

Now I don't care who you might have thought that you were and whomever you might want to be. But one thing that I always hated was when a nigga called one of my girls a bitch or a hoe, or even a sleuth. You see women who chose being a stripper for their profession would always get a bad reputation if they didn't fuck a broke ass brother or if they did! You see it's like this: If a female says to a guy who wants to fuck her, while she's shaking her ass for some cash, "I don't kick my game like that. All I'm here for is to dance and make my money!" The guy would always come back at her with, "Well, bitch, why are you in here taking off your clothes, if you don't want to fuck for some cash?"

My answer to the lame ass brother who would call strippers hoes and bitches, or sleuths was, "If she doesn't do what you guys wanted her to do, she would become one of these names that you decided to call her, when she was just trying to make an honest living."

I was getting a little upset with this lil' snotty nose punk who was calling out my girls because they wasn't fucking his ass. I had just calmed down as I asked him, "What's up, and what seems to be the problem that you have with my females?"

"Let's just step outside for a quick minute homie!" he said to me while ushering me out the backdoor of the spot.

I wanted to hit him in the back of his head as we walked outside, but I was trying to maintain my cool, because I didn't know what was about to take place and I sure as hell didn't want to stop my girls from making their money.

Damn, here we go, he wanted to talk to me about my ladies. What if his lil' ugly ass pulled out some fire? I said to myself as I got further and further out that door. Sexy Redd wasn't there to watch my back and my damn cousin was inside playing pool with his smoking partner.

As the both of us got outside, he had another dude sitting off to the side of the spot in a lawn chair. Then the guy who walked me outside turned around to me and said, "Yo cuz, I don't know you and shit, but I'm going to need for you to give me back all the money that my partner gave to you earlier. And you can take these no fucking ass hoes and your lil' black ass the fuck up out of here!"

I was looking around stunned and saying to myself, *Now I thought that I told the one nigga that my girls wasn't fucking?*

Then this nigga who was doing all the talking pulled out a fucking AK-47 with the banana clip. My eyes got big ass pancakes as I said to myself, *Damn, I'm about to die over some butt naked ass girls. Oh no, this shit is not supposed to happening to me! That's exactly what I get for not bringing my brother. Fuck! And Richard was still inside playing pool!*

Then this nigga points the barrel right in my face and said, "If you want that nice ass shirt of yours wet the fuck up we can do that, or you can just empty those fat ass pockets of yours and we can forget that this shit ever went down like this!"

CHAPTER 20
HE'S NOT A PIMP!

I looked around weighing my options, thinking of what I had gotten myself into, calculating my next move, before I was about to be blown away over some butt naked ass females. I was baffled at my situation. That's when I looked the guy directly in his eyes and said, "Fuck that, you can have his money back and all the extra money I have made throughout the night!" I was just about to take my money out of my pocket when I heard the music playing over the sound system.

The song was *Back To Life* by Soul to Soul. My heart stopped for just a mere second when out of nowhere I heard my sister's words playing through my mind. "You need them for your protection!" I then looked up like in slow motion to see a red dot on the forehead of the one guy who had the AK-47 pointed at me.

His lil' homie that was sitting off inside the lawn chair immediately shouted out to him. "Hey, KB, you have a red dot on your big ass forehead!"

KB then shouted back at his partner in crime, "Yo, Tay, you have one on your chest, my nigga!"

That's when I looked at KB standing there with that dot on his forehead, looking like a black Arab, and uttered, "Looks like we have ourselves a slight problem."

Seconds later is when I heard her voice resonating throughout the morning breeze. "Yep, that's exactly what we have here, Michael, and if these two knuckle heads want to ever see their families again, they better put their weapons down right now! Before we get this party started for real!" Nicole recited as she walked up behind me and then whispered in my ear, "Murder Queens on deck. We gotcha back, Mike."

Boy was I ever glad to see them females pull up on me like that.

I quickly turned to my left to witness Mignon listlessly walking down the stairs yelling, "Nah, forget putting down your weapons. I feel like killing me a nigga this morning anyway! So, make a move nigga so that I can shoot you right between them small ass eyes inside of your big ass head!"

As soon as she spoke those words, the one dude sitting inside the lawn chair jumped up and shouted, "Man, I didn't have anything to do with this shit! I'm gone!"

"If you don't sit your short, ugly black ass back down, you're gonna end up getting your lil' dumb ass shot right in your ugly ass face!" Strawberry— yeah, that's right; Strawberry— shouted at the lil' nigga as he started pissing on himself from being scarred shitless.

All of a sudden, the guy who had orchestrated the whole entire party emerged, fleetly walking downstairs all excited and nervous. He saw what was about to take place and yelled out to his friend KB. "Yo, what in the hell is going on? What are you fucking doing, KB?"

KB still had the AK-47 in his hand as he barked back at his partner, "Man these hoes ain't fucking nothing, so I wanted the money back!"

His partner looked over at him with fright written all over his face and shouted back at him with, "Man, I told your stupid ass before these females came over here that there would not be any money for sex involved! Mike doesn't play that shit, man. He's not a fucking pimp, dumb ass nigga!"

CHAPTER 21
OUT OF HERE

The guy who had paid us to come to their spot then looked at me with a sincere look on his face and said, "Mike I'm so sorry that he tried you like this!"

KB still had the weapon in his hand when Nicole looked at him and mumbled, "Nigga you have two seconds to put that AK down or I'm gonna make today your last day. No, better yet, give that shit to my girl standing right there."

Before he could even let it go, his homie was trying to give his weapon to Strawberry, when we are heard a very loud boom.

"Aw man, this bitch shot me in my fucking leg," his partner Tay shouted with a fucked-up expression on his fat ass face.

We all looked over at the young man sprawled out over the ground to see Strawberry standing over him. She looked up at us and then said, "My bad. That's the nigga who had his finger up in my ass earlier when I was dancing." She then looked down at the nigga who was grimacing in pain on the ground and angrily recited, "Now nigga, how does that shit feel? I hope it hurts just as much as it did when you had your nasty ass finger stuck up my tight asshole, with those long ass, dirty ass nails. I should've shitted on your nasty, ugly ass!" *WAAAAP!* She then slapped the shit out of his ass, as he laid there holding his swollen cheek, moaning in agonizing pain.

"Ok, well now that this is all over with, I think that I'm gonna get my ladies and get the hell out of here!" I voiced while looking at my beautiful females who had just rescued me.

The guy who had set up the party then asked me, "Damn Mike, where in the hell did you get these ladies from? They dance too?"

Nicole quickly cut in with, "Why of course we dance,

but we also make sure that the girls and Mr. Michael Vallentino are safe at all times!

A slight smile came across their faces as Strawberry looked over at me and voiced, "Let's go Mike, before I change my mind and shoot that one big headed ass nigga who had the AK-47 pointed at you. It's just something about his lil' sneaky ass that I don't like. He just seems like the grimy type!"

I was briskly walking right behind the girls as I yelled out, "Yeah, let's ride, Murder Queens." I then took a brief sigh of relief after I had realized how important those girls were to me and the group. They had saved my life that particular morning.

Three weeks later those same two low-life ass niggas who tried to rob me were found dead somewhere in Tampa, Florida. The news reported that they had tried to rob a group of dancers one early mid-morning after a bachelor party. The Florida Hot Girls were not at the show, but them damn Murder Queens were spotted leaving the show in quite a hurry. The case still remains a cold case to this very day. If you ask me the Murder Queens didn't have anything to do with it. That's my story and that's what I'm sticking with!

When I got back inside of the spot, Richard was still over in the corner playing pool. He spotted me coming through the side door and shouted out to me, "Hey, cuz, where you been," while pulling out his blunt and blowing out billows of smoke.

I angrily looked at him. "Man, what the fuck ever! Get the girls together. We're out of here!" I said to Richard with a fierce tone in my voice, as I was directing the ladies to get dressed as well; before KB called up some of his homies and then we would've really had an intense gun battle in the streets of St. Pete.

CHAPTER 22
BET MONEY ON THAT SHIT!

Richard was walking back out of the girls' makeshift dressing room when he looked at me and asked me, "Cuz, what's going on? Why are we leaving all of a sudden?"

I angrily turned to him and barked, "Man, them niggas was about to kill me outside and your ass was up in here playing pool with Chief Smoking Head Chazz!"

His dry mouth fell wide open. "Mike, I thought that you were outside with Divia!"

"How, when Divia has been in here with you all while I was outside with a damn AK-47 pointed at my dome! Get the females so that we can get the hell out of here!"

While standing there telling him what had happened, the girls were running past us screaming, "Mike, what's up, what in the hell happened?" Some of them didn't even have on all their clothing while running outside to the different trucks that they came in.

I was standing in between the two vehicles by now when Peaches, who was one of the new chicks from Orlando, ran up on me half naked. I looked at her with an inquisitive stare on my face, due to her being half naked standing there with her ass cheeks hanging out of her outfit. "Now what in the hell were you doing that has half of your ass hanging out your fucking outfit?"

She was all nervous and scarred as she looked up at me and uttered while shaking like a leaf on a tree, "I wasn't doing nothing Mike, I swear," while I was facing her talking with her ass being partially naked.

This guy walked up behind me yelling, "Oh hell naw! I just paid for some ass, now somebody is going to knock this dick back down!"

I turned around to see this shirtless nigga standing behind me with a rock-hard dick protruding from his Dickie

57

pants. I wittily turned back to Ms. Peaches fast ass, who was still behind me screaming, "I wasn't doing nothing, I swear!"

A smirk darted across my face as I said, "Well, whoever was in there with his half-horse, half-man looking ass needs to go back inside and finish whatever you were about to do!"

Peaches then looked around at the females who were all inside their respectful vehicles looking back at her, as if she thought that one of the other girls were going back inside with him to handle all that pressure. Once she saw that no one was moving, she then looked up at me with both of her eyes looking like an extra-large Pizza from Papa Johns. "Y'all ain't going to leave me here, are you? Because Orlando is a real long fucking walk from here!"

I stared back at her and yelled, "Girl, hurry your lying ass the fuck up!"

The other females started laughing as she ran back inside the spot behind the dude who she was with.

Suga Bear poked her head out of the truck and shouted out at her, while her outfit tried to hang onto her fine ass, "I hope your ass got paid well for all that dick you are about to have to deal with!"

Peaches' best friend Coca then replied to Suga Bear, "My girl is a real trooper. She's going to knock all that dick down in about fifteen minutes! We can bet money on that shit!"

CHAPTER 23
OUR LIVES

Peekachu just had to chimed in with her two cents as she looked at Coca and said, "Yeah, and watch her ass limps the fuck back out to this truck and pass the fuck out, because that nigga looked like he was part elephant or something with all that meat he was packing between his legs!"

I looked over at Richard, who was sitting in the driver's seat of his truck, still somewhat high from the herbal essence that he had been smoking on with Chazz. "Yo Richard, you have all of your girls with you, right?"

"Yeah, cuz, every one of my girls are here and accounted for!"

"Cool. Y'all go ahead and leave, we'll catch up with you all down the road. There is no need for y'all to have to wait on us. I thought that I told all of you girls that there was no VIP shit going on tonight. But since she decided to try my gangsta, I'm going to have to deal with her my way!"

"Alright, cousin. We're out of here!" Richard shouted as he started up the truck.

"Yeah, drive safe, and I'll get with you sometime tomorrow."

He shot me the piece sign and then backed out with his females wanting to stay with us, so that they could be nosey. Richard pulled off with one of his girls in the back seat still yelling, "What in the hell happened? Why did we have to leave? We were just about to get more money?"

Richard bent a left headed to I-275. He told me later that whatever female was sitting in the front seat stepped on the weapon that KB had in his hand that night, and answered the young ladies question with, "Somebody said that the Murder Queens showed up and shut the muthafucker down; that's why we had to leave! Here is one of their weapons right here. My ass just stepped on it!"

"No, it isn't, silly ass girl. That belongs to one of the

niggas who tried to rob Mike outside!" Richard replied.

"Damn, them niggas were trying to rob Mike?"

"Not all of them, just some nigga who was mad that you all weren't fucking Chazz!" Richard replied.

Chyna turned around staring back at where she had just came from and shouted up to Richard, "Yo, Rich, turn this damn truck around! I want to see who the Murder Queens are!"

Rich said that he looked up in his rear-view mirror and shouted back at her, "Mike told me to get you girls back home to Orlando safely! If you want to find out who they are, you're going to have to find that out on your own!" *Hell, I want to find that out too. Maybe they know who's responsible for killing my baby's mother,* Richard said to himself as he merged onto I-275.

Just as he merged, Chyna turned back up front and whispered out loud, "Damn, Mike. When they all get back in Orlando, I'm going to find out just who them females are. I need them to handle something for me."

"Good luck with that. Either way, Mike said that he didn't know who those females are," Tiny uttered as she sat there looking out the window and sorting out her money at the same time.

"Whatever. Mike knows who those females are. His slick ass just isn't telling us. And besides, how is it that they always show up and somehow save his life? Come to think of it, all of our lives!"

"You do have a point there, Chyna!"

CHAPTER 24
JAIL

The girls and I sat there for about another fifteen minutes, and just like Coca had stated earlier, Peaches was coming back to the truck. And just like Peekachu had stated, she was limping. As far as sleeping? Hell naw. None of us did. I was tired and drained from a very long night and day, so when I asked someone to drive for me, The lil' precious, adorable Ms. Sweetness volunteered to drive us all back home.

Now as I remembered, I had specifically asked her lil' cute, red ass at least three times. "Do you have license?"

Her answer every time was the exact same thing. "Yes, Michael, I have my driver's license. Just sit back and enjoy the ride back home, sweetheart." She would always answer with that, reassuring me that everything would be okay.

As I sat back and placed my weary head on the headrest of my black 2000 Yukon Denali, my black ass should have at least asked to see her license, because the cops were sure as hell going to ask to see it just as soon as we got pulled over.

I had just eased my head back into a comfortable position when I began evaluating my situation, from the group of females that I had in the group, to my cousin who I had working for me. To even having Ms. Divia by my side as my new ride or die chick. Where was I taking the girls and how far could I actually take my beautiful flock of exotic women. Sexy Redd was gone, and the gorgeous, sexy ass Nicole was constantly trying to become a significant part of my confused, out of control life. She had already showed me that she would kill for me, and with an attitude like that from that type of female, was more of a negative than a positive. Last but not the least was the constant thought of me fathering two more kids out of wedlock and practically at the same damn time. Every time that I even tried to think of anything besides my Florida Hot Girls, my mind would go blank. It seemed as though the Florida Hot Girls had some type of hold on me and my life. Basically all I wanted to do was go make money each and every night, no matter what.

I had my head all the way back on the headrest, trying to doze off to sleep, while trying to make sense of everything, all while Ms. Sweetness was driving like she was involved in some type of high-speed race to get us back to Orlando. I raised my head up to look over at Divia sitting next to me.

She saw that I was looking at her and looked back at me with a pleasant smile covering her face and said, "Michael, don't you think that ole girl is driving a bit too fast?"

"I was just about to ask you the same thing, beautiful," I replied as I leaned up in my seat and tapped the back of the driver's seat. "Hey, could you please slow down a tad bit? We're going to get pulled over as fast as you're driving, young lady," I said to Sweetness while adjusting myself back in my seat, at the same time thinking to myself, *Hell, I have three arrest warrants on my ass and I sure as hell don't want to go to jail today!*

CHAPTER 25
RHYNYIA SANTIAGO

Linda, the new chick from Haines City, along with this other chick from Dothan, Alabama by the name of Lexus were both sitting in the front seat of the vehicle with Sweetness.

When Linda saw that Sweetness was driving over the speed limit as well, she turned to me sitting behind them and motioned with her lips, "Mike, I have a warrant, so we can't get pulled over!"

I started looking around the truck wondering who else had a warrant. Whomever had one besides Linda and I were about to find out as fast as this lil' heifer was driving my truck that early mid-morning.

No one said anything as she kept right on speeding down I-4. The rest of the crew all pretended to be fast asleep, but with their eyes partly opened. It seemed as though everyone was off in a daze. I was still nervous as this chick wasn't letting off the gas at all. It was as if she wanted to get pulled over as she sped in and out of traffic headed to Orlando. The speed limit was 75 miles-per-hour and this female was doing at least 100. She had just passed the Dover exit on I-4 with her lil' small head looking straight ahead. And then it happened. Out of nowhere came those flashing blue and red lights.

"Fuck, I told your black ass to slow the fuck down! Now we about to get pulled the fuck over!" I yelled at her as she acted as if she didn't hear anything I had just said to her ass. *Well, it was nice while it lasted. Now my black ass is about to go to jail. Damn, I told this pie-faced ass girl to slow her lil' red ass down! Now I'm about to get thrown in jail, I said to myself while she was still driving down the interstate with the police right behind us.*

I was a bit relived that we had the girls place that damn AK-47 in the other truck, because if we would have got caught with that, we would have been charged with everybody linked to that damn weapon.

Linda started to panic as Sweetness kept right on speeding down the road without pulling over and with the cop still chasing right behind us.

"Aw, hell naw! This bitch has us on a high-speed chase on I-4! Man we're about to be on the morning news. Girl, pull this muthafucka over! What do you have going on? Whatever it is, we don't want any part of it," Lexus shouted to her while looking back at the number of cops chasing us, with this crazy ass chick still driving as if she didn't realize that we were even being chased by at least three patrol cars.

After about another intense, terrifying ten minutes of trying to elude the police, she finally decided to pull over, with everyone inside the truck like, "Damn, bitch! Why in the hell were you driving so damn fast in the first place?" She just sat there not mumbling a word to anyone, as if she was in a trance or deep coma.

"Hey, do you hear us talking to you?" I yelled at her with still no answer.

She just continued to sit there motionless as if she were retarded or something. Meanwhile, the lead officer who had pulled us over was still sitting inside of his patrol car reading the tag before he approached the window.

I laid my head back and said a silent prayer to myself, not worrying about the tag or registration, since the vehicle was registered in the name of Rhynyia "Sexy Redd" Santiago. Boy, how I wished for her presence at that very moment.

CHAPTER 26
TECH NINES

I was sitting in the back seat of the Denali, watching, and waiting for the officer to walk up to the window. Three minutes into watching and waiting to see what he was going to do, he slowly got out of his patrol car and marched towards to the driver side window, trying to see how many people were actually sitting inside the vehicle.

It seemed as though we were all in a horror movie, waiting on the monster to kill us, as we sat there nervously waiting on this fucking cop. Before he got closer to the vehicle, I looked throughout the vehicle at the women and then shouted throughout the truck, "Okay, listen up closely, ladies. Everybody just remain calm and let her crazy ass answer any questions that he wants to ask!"

Poor scared to death ass Linda turned to stare at me sitting in the back seat with crocodile tears running down her face, as she hollered, "Mike, this bitch ain't saying nothing and she's just sitting here like her ass is about to go into some type of shock or something!"

I quickly turned to Coca and cried. "Coca, this is your friend! What in the hell is wrong with her crazy ass?"

Coca looked over at me with an uncertain look on her face and replied, "I don't know Mike. She ain't talking to my ass either."

"Fuck, man, I don't want to go to jail this morning or any other morning. I knew that I should've drove!" I yelled to the truckload of girls as we all were sitting there waiting on the cop to come to the vehicle.

Two minutes later he walked up and tapped on the truck window. *Bing, Bing, Bing!* Sweetness just sat there still looking straight ahead as the cop continued to tap on the window. It was as if she didn't even see the damn cop knocking on the window, while everyone else inside the vehicle was yelling at her to let down the window.

"Girl, let the fucking window down before the cop starts shooting up inside this bitch ass truck!" Linda shouted at her.

"Aw man, Mike I think your girl is about to do something real stupid up here in this fucking front seat!" Lexus shouted to me as she placed her head down between her knees and started praying to the Almighty one upstairs.

What in the hell is really going? Was this bitch losing her mind, and why did I have to let her dumb ass drive in the first place, I said to myself as I just put my head back on the headrest.

That's when Nicole whispered in my ear from the back seat next to Mignon, Strawberry and the one skinny black chick Michelle, "Mike, me and the rest of the Murder Queens are strapped. We can shoot our way out of this bitch if you want to. Just as long as we get your black ass out of here alive, we're good."

"What?" I asked her with a frantic ass look over my frightened face.

"Yeah, Mike. We're ready to die."

"Nicole, please. What in the hell are you females? Some real professional hired hit women?"

She looked at me with a chaotic, deranged ass look on her face. "We're ready to die for ours at any given time," she said as she looked over at the rest of her girls who all looked like they were getting ready for a gunfight.

I quickly peered over to witness Ms. Strawberry placing a silencer on the barrel of this long ass pistol that I could have sworn she pulled out of her pussy. I was like, *Damn, how long is that barrel on that damn pistol that you just pulled out of that big ass pussy of yours?* She just smiled back at me as Mignon and Entyce pulled out some weapons that looked just like Tech Nines.

CHAPTER 27
OPRAH WINFREY

I was tripping at the sight of what was transpiring right in front of my black ass, when I shouted out in the direction of Nicole, "C'mon, man. I'm not in a fucking western movie am I?" I was staring in the direction of all four of the Murder Queens, while the officer was still trying to get Ms. Stuck on Stupid to let her window down.

By now he was shouting and screaming, telling her to let down the window, when she gracefully obliged and started rolling the window down slowly. Just as she had got the window halfway down she started screaming at the top of her lungs back at the cop, who stepped back and drew his weapon, fearing for his life.

That's when I heard the Murder Queens shout, "Die, muthafucker, die!"

I fucking fainted right before they could pop off any rounds, as the cop pulled out his revolver and shouted at Sweetness, "Out of the vehicle right now, with your hands up!"

Nicole and the rest of the Murder Queens slid their weapons back where they had retrieved them from, while Divia was whispering over me, "Mike, are you okay?"

I was breathing all hard as I looked back at her and said, "Man, what in the fuck just happened?"

"Nigga, your black ass passed out!" Nicole shouted as she slapped me across my face and voiced, "Get a fucking grip nigga and pull yourself together. Hell I was just about to put a hole in that cop's fucking wig!"

While Nicole was thrashing me with her words, the cop was placing Sweetness' red ass in the backseat of his patrol car. Seconds later we saw more cops start to arrive to help assist him.

Linda who was scarred half to death by now turned to the passengers who were sitting in the backseat looking at all the officers and said, "Hey, it was nice dancing with you guys. Guess I'll be seeing you guys after I get out of jail, thanks to fucking Speed Racer."

That's when one of the other officers walked up to the truck and poked her head inside. "Good morning. Do you all have your IDs on you?" the short-built white female officer asked the truckload of us.

"Aw, no, I don't have my ID with me!" I said to her while shaking like a leaf on a tree.

She quickly came back with. "Okay, sir, well what's your name please?"

I knew damn well if I gave her my full government name I was good as gone, so I gave her the name, "Andre Miller, ma'am."

She wrote it down as Linda heard the fake name that I had just whispered to the officer and decided to give her one as well.

"Your name, ma'am?"

Linda looked back at me and smiled as she uttered to the female officer, "Oprah Winfrey, ma'am. My name is Oprah Winfrey!"

We all looked around at one another. *Damn, not Oprah Winfrey, Linda.*

The rest of the ladies all produced their IDs as the officer replied, "Okay. You guys give me a quick minute while I run your IDs. it will only take a minute."

Everyone let out a sigh of relief as she walked back to her patrol car. The tension in the air was so thick that you could have cut it with a knife, when Coca uttered out loud, "I don't think that ole girl has a driver's license!"

CHAPTER 28
MICHAEL

I had just turned back around from looking to see what was going on inside the officer's patrol car when I said to Coca, "Thanks, Coca. It's too late now. Do you have a valid driver's license?"

"Yes," she answered sarcastically.

"Well, why didn't your ass drive?"

"Hell, she jumped her hot, fast ass in the front seat like she wanted to drive!"

While her and I went back and forth debating about who should have drove, the officer came back to the truck and said, "Do you all mind if I search the vehicle?"

I knew that there weren't any drugs in the vehicle, so I quickly answered, "No, sir, you go right ahead and do your job, officer."

We all stepped out and walked in the middle of the highway, since Sweetness had pulled over on the wrong side which had us standing on the median.

The police dogs were walking around the vehicle smelling for drugs when I looked amongst the females standing there with me and said, "Hey, someone is missing. Where is the lil' slim black chick Michelle that was sitting in the back seat with you all, Strawberry?"

"She was there a minute ago. Maybe she vanished up into thin air!" Strawberry replied with sarcasm in her voice.

"Very funny Strawberry."

"Naw, I'm serious Mike. Wait a minute, she may have left when your punk ass fainted. Or better yet, after my girl Nicole slapped the shit out of your scary ass!"

"Alright Strawberry, just because you can pull a six-inch barrel out of your extra-large pussy, doesn't mean that you can talk to me any kind of way."

She looked back at me and then replied, "Well, it wouldn't be extra-large if your wild and crazy ass brother wouldn't have been trying to stand up inside of it."

We were all still stunned as to how this lil' skinny, dark ass female had disappeared just like that without any signs of her nowhere in sight.

"Damn, did she run in the woods when we were all getting out of the truck?"

"Don't know, Mike, if she did or not. We all can honestly say that she must've got away. Or maybe she was a ghost or something."

Strawberry continued to answer my questions with dumb ass answers, when I came back at her with, "Strawberry, when we get back, I'm taking your crazy ass to the doctor to have you checked out, because if I can get a check for your crazy ass, I'm all in!"

"Whatever. Mike."

The officer started to walk back towards us as he said, "Okay, your vehicle is clean and you guys are free to go!"

"Thank you, sir!"

It was music to my ears until I heard the officer say to me, "Hold on there for a second, sir."

"Who, me?" I said while standing there about to turn into a world-class sprinter.

"Yes," he said as I knew I was toast. "Sir, you say that your name is Andre Miller, correct?"

I looked up into his cold blue eyes as I answered, sounding like a runaway slave, "Yesum, that's bees my name, sir!"

I was shaking like a leaf on a tree in the middle of December, when he said, "Well the young lady in the back seat of my patrol car says that your name is Michael!"

CHAPTER 29
WHAT I HAD CREATED

I was really shaking by now. My legs were moving so fast back and forth, that I had started thinking back to my old high school track days. I actually heard a gun go off in my head as I thought it was the starter pistol, letting me know that the race had begun. My knees had bent on their own as I started to sprint down the road, running at top speed to get away from the cops that morning. But just as my luck would have it, I happened to look over at the truckload of beautiful women that I had. They were all looking out of the window, staring at me as if they were watching a movie. That's when I weighed my options and decided to stay put right there and face the music.

Seconds later is when the officer asked me, "So, you're telling me that if I take you downtown, your prints are going to come back Andre Miller?"

I was scared and nervous as hell when I replied, "Yep, that's what's going to come back, officer. Andre Miller."

He took his hand down from my chest, allowing me to pass and then politely uttered, "Alright, Mr. Miller, you're free to go."

I was elated as I ran back towards my truck.

The girls were all ready to go as smiles were beaming from each one of their faces. Sweetness was the only female that wasn't inside the truck as we all were looking around for her. Then out of nowhere she popped up trying to get back in the front seat, as she thought that she was still about to drive us home.

Everybody yelled out to her ass, "Hell naw! You drive too fast, and we don't want to die at your hands."

Coca pushed her lil' red ass out of the driver's seat. "I got it. Sit back and get yourself some sleep!"

Just as Coca pulled off, the lil' black chick Michelle rolled back over from the backseat.

"Where in the hell were you at?" I barked at her as she was looking like she had been sleeping the whole entire time that we all where outside of my truck.

She looked back at me with those big ass eyes of hers and said, "Man, I'm riding so dirty Mike, that I had to hide because if them crackers would have found all this weed on me, I would have been riding in the backseat of one of them patrol cars!"

We all laughed all the way back to Orlando. That is, everyone except Sweetness. She rode all the way back as if she were still stuck in some type of shock. The ride home that early mid Monday morning answered my question as to if this is what I wanted in my complexed life. And was this my destiny as far as it being something that I would do until the day I died. I had escaped the long arm of the law one more time, but little did I know, it would all come to an abrupt halt with the help of a few bitches who I would let enter my domain. In other words, I would let the wrong individuals join my elite group of beautiful women. And once I had decided to let them go after I found out their true identities, they in turn would try to destroy what I had created.

CHAPTER 30
WAKE UP DIVIA

It was a nice, pleasant, beautiful Monday morning as I rolled out of bed, ready to start my day. I had once again averted the long arm of the law and was electrified to be rolling out of my big ass bed, while Ms. Divia laid there stretched out, butt bunky-ass naked.

You see, after we had finally made it back that morning, I had to get some unwanted stress off of my head. And your girl Ms. Divia was more than happy to help me relieve all the previous day's problems off of my mind. So, she had been up half the morning while trying to help me alleviate all that unwanted stress that I had.

The time was around 11:30AM as I walked downstairs to prepare breakfast for the large house full of people that I had living with me. While preparing some bacon, country sausage, hash browns and grits, along with some big ass grandma pancakes, your girl Nicole walked her half naked, sexy ass body around the corner of the kitchen.

She saw me busy at work as she said, "Good morning, Michael." She was standing there with nothing on but her lace, see through night gown and a pair of nice bright red thongs that she wore like a fucking glove while half of her bare pussy hung from the right side of them.

"Morning, Nicole," I replied while trying not to look at how nice she looked in her outfit.

"What? Are you cooking breakfast for all of us?"

I shyly looked up at her and replied, "Yes, Nicole. Why, are you hungry?"

"Yes, I am, Michael, but what I want is not in that skillet that your cooking in. I want that sausage between your legs," she said with a smile on her pleasurable red face, as she snatched a piece of bacon off the platter and then placed it inside of her mouth, working it as if it was my swollen manhood stuffed deep down her throat.

I gave her a nonchalant smile and then said, "Girl, you just don't quit, do you?"

"Nope. Why should I? To me, you're fair game now, and I'm not going to stop until I get what I want!"

I placed the hot skillet in the sink as I said to her, "C'mon, Nicole. Now you know that Divia is still upstairs and if she finds out that you're down here trying to give me some of that good ass pussy of yours, it's going to be trouble around here!"

She just looked back at me and asked, "When is she leaving anyway Michael? I'm getting tired of waiting on what's mine." She sat her nice, round, red ass on one of the bar stools as she continued to watch me prepare breakfast. I was pretending not to hear her as she continued rambling. "Hell, Michael, I waited for Ms. Kitty to leave, then I waited for Sexy Redd to leave. I'm getting tired of waiting. I want some dick and I want it right muthafucking now! Now when are you going to fuck me, Michael?"

I dropped the spatula and ran around the kitchen counter with my index finger over my mouth. "Shhh! You're gonna wake up Divia," I recited to her with my finger still up to my mouth, but it was too late.

Divia then stepped around the corner of the foyer with a fucked up unit over her face. "Don't worry, Michael, she already has!"

CHAPTER 31
DAMN!

I could see the fire and animosity in the burning eyes of my dear Divia as she stood there with her hands on her hips for about thirty seconds before looking over at me and saying, "Michael, please call me a cab to take me to the Greyhound bus station! I know when I'm not wanted. And besides, I have my two kids back home to attend to. I don't have time to be around here battling with some chick over some dick, no matter how good it is!"

Nicole swiftly pulled her night gown around her half naked body and looked back Divia and me, smiling as to what she had started.

That's when I moved a bit closer to Divia and placed my hands on her shoulders and whispered into her ear, "Hey, wait a minute, boo. Don't let her get to you. She's been like that ever since Sexy Redd left to go back home."

Divia looked back up into my eyes with a tear snaking down her right cheek and uttered. "I know, Michael, she told me everything yesterday. Listen, I'm not here trying to fight another female over you, and besides all of that, who and where is your so-called main lady, Sexy Redd?"

I was stuck. I couldn't say anything as Divia just stood there with tears slowly running down both sides of her beautiful face. I couldn't lie to her, so I simply answered her with, "Alright, Divia, I'll take you back home instead of you catching the bus. I'll have the limo take us back. Go ahead and get your things together while I make the call."

She turned her back to me and walked towards the stairs as I stood there staring at just how fine she was. Just as she had reached the bottom of the staircase, she turned back to me and voiced, "Michael, I'll be back. Just let me get things together back in Gainesville. Once things are good with my kids and you have your head on straight, I'll come back to you and this wild and crazy ass group of girls that you have." She cut a half smile back at me and then hurried upstairs.

I was a bit relieved that she was going home because I knew after a few days of her being up under me would cause me to lose interest. I just didn't want her to be leaving on behalf of Nicole's wild and jealous ass.

With Divia back upstairs I went to make the call to the limo service, but just as I went into my pocket to grab my phone it began ringing. I had just pulled it out of my pocket to see that it was Sharon calling me. "Hello."

"Mike!" She sounded hysterical as though something very bad had happened.

"Yes, Sharon," I said back into the phone, not knowing what to expect next.

"He's missing!" she screamed into the phone, sounding like she was crying.

"Who's missing, bae?" I asked her, trying to sound concerned.

"My uncle Bernard. Fats!" she screamed into the phone all loud and frenzied.

I was stuck in between a rock and a hard place as I sat there listening to the way she was crying in the background. "Damn, what happened to him? And are you sure he's missing?" I asked her, trying to sound as if I fucking cared about his fat, black, nasty, thirsty ass.

"I don't know, Michael. My mom just called me and told me the bad news!"

"Okay, Sharon, just calm down. When was the last time you saw or even spoke to him?" I asked her while falling down into my sofa when she hit me with what I didn't want to hear.

"It was Friday, right before you guys left. He came by my house with some female he said that he had met from Miami. Talking about how he wanted me to meet her!"

I placed my hand over my head and fell even further into my couch, while screaming, "Damn!"

CHAPTER 32
LEAVE FOR GAINESVILLE

Damn, how could this had happened, I said to myself right before Sharon said, "But before I could put on some clothes and run out to see her sitting outside in his car, he said that she had to go check into her hotel room before three or she would lose her reservation!"

I took a sigh of relief as I sat there calculating my next move without Sharon knowing that I had anything to do with his disappearance. I sat there tentatively thanking to myself what else could go wrong and thanking God that she didn't see Yani or get a good look at her at all. I had already been responsible for taking out her lil' grimy ass cousin Do-Dirty. Now here I was trying to console her after giving the order to cancel her thirsty ass uncle. I continued sitting there listening to her vent about how he had come by with Yani when I thought to just tell her what her people were trying to do to me and my empire of beautiful exotic women. My problems would be over, and the both of us could just move away and start our lives over. It wouldn't be that easy. She would probably try to extort me next.

So, as she finished talking just long enough to catch her breath, I was like, "Okay, listen, boo. I have to leave for a few hours. There is some small business that I have to take care of in Gainesville."

"But Michael, I need you here with me. You told me that when you returned from the road that you would be here for me."

"I know Sharon, but this is important."

"And so is this, Michael. I need you here with me. And if it's so damn important, why can't I just go with you?"

"Sharon."

"Michael!" I could tell by her tone that I wasn't going to win that one. She wasn't taking no for an answer. In other words, she was very determined to travel to Gainesville with me.

"Alright, I won't go. It will just have to wait until later. Let me hop in the shower. Give me about an hour and I'll be over to see you in a bit!"

"Michael," she said sounding like she missed me.

"Yes, Sharon," I said sounding like I missed her more.

"I love you!" If she only knew what I had done and what I was capable of doing.

"I love you, too." I hung up the phone just as Divia stepped into the living room with more tears jumping off of her face.

She stared at me and then shouted, "Damn, you're just full of surprises, huh, Mr. Michael Vallentino?"

"Naw Divia, it's not like that. It just seems to be the start of a very interesting day."

She then placed her index finger over my lips before I lied to her, and she knew that it was going to be a lie. "I understand, Michael. You have a lot of things to take care of and I am aware of just how busy you are." She was standing there talking to me with her nice ass camel toe protruding out of her spandex bicycle shorts. She must have seen my eyes staring at how nice it looked to me when she uttered, "Oh you want the pussy now, huh? Your black whoreish ass can forget about my tight ass pussy and me! When does the limo get here?" Her smile turned into a frown.

CHAPTER 33
TURNING INTO!

I looked up at her, standing there wiping her face, still being angry at me. "I haven't had a chance to call them yet."

She then sucked her teeth as she sat down across from me, staring out of the window.

I pulled my phone out and hit the number nine on my keypad, which was the speed dial for Prestige Limo Service.

The phone rung one time before the lovely voice on the other line answered. "Prestige Limo Service, how can we help you today?"

"Yes, can I please speak to Preston?"

"Yes sir, can I tell him who's calling?"

"Yes, it's Michael Vallentino."

"Oh, hello Mr. Vallentino," the receptionist said to me, sounding too excited to know that it was me on the phone. I could hear her yell out, "Preston! It's Mr. Vallentino on line one!"

He picked up. "Well, hello, my dear friend."

"Hello, Preston. How in the hell are you?"

"I was fine until some detectives dropped by here a few days ago, asking questions about the limo I rented out to you."

"What?" I asked while standing up.

"Yes, they were saying that one of my limos were seen at the ole paper mill on the day it exploded with those poor souls inside."

"Damn, how could that be?" I asked sounding confused and very concerned.

"I know, tell me about it. Michael, you sure that you guys didn't have anything to do with that horrible incident?"

"Not at all, Preston. Where is that particular limo parked at right now?" I asked now sounding as if there was something wrong.

"I have it parked at one of our storage units out of the

public's eye."

"Okay, listen, keep it there. And do you have anyone available to take one of my females to Gainesville?"

"Yes, I'll have Tristan at your house immediately," he said.

"Thanks, I'll handle everything else in about two days!"

"Thank you, Michael."

"No problem, Preston. I'll talk with you later."

As soon as I hung up with Preston, Divia was standing there in my face. "Michael, what are you into besides the dancers?"

I looked back at her with a cold blank stare on my face and answered, "Divia, my business is my business. Now that's all I'm going to say about that! Now are you packed and ready to leave?"

She backed away slowly and then softly uttered, "Yes, Michael. Excuse me for trying to be there for you. I won't ever ask you of your other business ventures again!"

I reached out and grabbed her arm before she turned to walk away, and simply replied, "It's not that, Divia. It's just that I have to be very careful when it comes to letting anyone get close to what I'm trying to accomplish here. Now the driver should be here in twenty minutes. I won't be able to ride back with you. Enjoy the ride home and I will see you when you return."

She stood firm in my face and replied, "Michael, I wish that you could have at least rode back home with me."

"You don't know how I wanted to, but something very important has come up that requires my immediate attention. I'm about to go upstairs to get a shower so that I can get across town. If you're gone by the time I get out, have a safe trip and call me as soon as you get home." I then turned my back to her and walked upstairs to my room, because I couldn't stand to see another female break down and cry over what the Florida Hot Girls were turning me into.

CHAPTER 34
BACK IN MY ARMS

As I stood there removing my clothing from my body, I happened to take a glance at myself in the mirror. And just for those few seconds I couldn't recognize the reflection staring back at me. I was changing. No longer was I that shy, compassionate young man that worked as a case manager for the State of Florida's welfare system. Nor was I that man who had married one of the most beautiful women that Orlando, Florida had to offer, by the name of Camisha J. I was now the man who was becoming a dog, a cheat, a man that only cared about one thing and one thing only, which was making my money and a lot of it, every single night. The days of wearing two-piece Armani suits to an office full of women needing my assistance with finding a job so that they wouldn't lose their welfare benefits were all behind me now.

I stared in that mirror at the man who wasn't driving a beat up white 1994 stinking Lincoln Continental to work every day. Now I was driving many different cars at any time that I wanted to. And I was living in a brand new $350,000 home, right dab smack in the middle of Metro West, with half of the Orlando Magic basketball team being my neighbors.

As I balled up my fist and slammed it down hard against my walnut stained dresser drawer, I shouted out, "Damn!" I then walked away from the mirror to witness Tristan opening the door for Divia to sit inside the nice white plush limo. *Damn, part of me was really going to miss her*, I thought.

My life and my world was changing, and I couldn't stop it. And even if I could, I don't think that I would have. Who was I fooling? I loved my life and my life loved me back. I was living any man's dream of beautiful women all around him at all times and with me being able to fuck anyone of them at any given moment.

I dully walked into my shower while removing my sports brief from my chiseled body frame that I had put so much work into while playing semi-pro football for the Lakeland Cowboys—a team in which I had took to three consecutive Semi-Pro Bowl Championships while being the quarterback. How I missed those days as I could only sit back and dream about the days of yester-year.

I was definitely changing into someone else now. I was becoming what some individuals in high level authority positions called a pimp. But to me, I was just a man who had a lot of women who wanted the same thing as me. Money, and a lot of it.

As the hot water pulsated off of my back, I heard the door to my bedroom open slowly as if the person who opened it didn't want me to hear them enter into my room. "Yeah? Who is it? I'm in the shower; give me a minute. I'll be right out!" I shouted from behind my bathroom door. There was no answer as the bathroom door opened, revealing a shadowy figure of a woman standing in my doorway. "Divia, is that you? I thought that you were gone!" I shouted, waiting for her to respond.

"Naw, my nigga. It isn't Divia; it's me," the voice that belonged to the silhouette shouted to me as the song by Silk *Back in My Arms* started playing in the background.

CHAPTER 35
I LOVE YOU TOO!

I was standing there with the water oscillating against my body as I waited for the person the voice belonged to, to emerge from behind the door. "Nicole!" I said as I seemed shocked, knowing that she was still hungry for more of what I had spoiled her with.

She emerged from behind the door butt ass naked, looking like a Playboy Bunny as she lazily walked into the shower with me and then placed her succulent lips on mine. She then placed her tongue so deep down my throat that I thought I was going to choke. I gently placed my hands on her tender-to-touch ass, as I welcomed her into the shower with me. Moments later my manhood was sticking out so far that she had to position herself around it just to stand in front of me.

She looked down at its nice size and stature and then mumbled to me while smiling, "See, I knew that you wanted me, Michael."

I then looked down at her gorgeous ass and replied with a smile, "Yes, I never said that I didn't. I just asked you to be patient. The moment would present itself eventually." I then picked her up and slid my erect manhood into her tight pussy, nice and slow. I could feel her take a deep breath and tense up as I began to go deeper and deeper into her wet womb, where no other man besides myself had ever been before.

She placed her arms around me as I placed her back up against the shower walls and started thrusting back and forth slowly as she uttered into my ear, "Michael Vallentino, I love you with all my heart. Please don't break it!"

I raised my head up from watching my manhood slide back and forth in between the lips of her pretty ass pussy, and replied, "I love you more, Nicole." It was in the heat of passion as I didn't realize what I was saying to her.

If only I would have known what I was creating at that very moment, maybe I would have never made love to her that particular day. I had crossed that fine line of heartbreak and betrayal, for betrayal is worse than death. I was about to break the heart of someone who would at any given moment risk or kill someone for the mere safety and well-being of my survival, without even thinking about her life in return. As I had said a many of times before, the only person or thing that I was in love with was the fact of me being married to what we all know as the Florida Hot Girls!

CHAPTER 36
COME HERE MA!

I took Nicole out of my shower, headed to my bed with my manhood still engulfed up in her small, frail stomach.

She was holding onto me as though I was the last man on the planet, as I gently laid her down on my bed with her looking directly into my eyes, watching her lips speak as she tediously uttered, "This is what I've been asking for since the first day that I laid my eyes upon you."

Me being cool and debonair as I was, looked back at her and simply replied, ever so gently, "I know, Nicole and you're just what I've been needing for the last few days of my ever so confusing life. Now hush and enjoy the time that we have between us."

The moment was intense just as it was exciting as both of our bodies were moving back and forth in sync with one another. In other words, she was throwing it back just like I liked it. I guess I had taught her well, as we both continued carrying on like two love birds deep in the moment of some abysmal, erotic passion.

Forty-five minutes later, we both lay there breathing hard and deep, when she rolled over and asked me, "So how was it, baby?"

"Naw, how was I, Nicole?" I replied to her with a question.

She then raised up in bed. "You were just as good as you were the very first time that you made love to me! Now once again, Mr. Michael, how was I," she asked me as she walked into the bathroom with her nice ass swaying from side to side.

"You know that your shit is the bomb, lil' lady. I don't know why you would even ask me that question. One thing for sure is that you really know how to make your pussy grab a nigga's dick. Don't cha?"

"Hell, every chick should know how to do that. All they

have to do is use their pussy muscles and just tighten them up around the dick!"

"So you're a pro at making love now I see?" I asked her as she placed a hot, soapy rag on my manhood and started washing me off.

She looked up at me while gently cleaning me off and asked me, "Mike, how long do you think that I've been fucking?"

I looked down at her and then began smiling at her, as I replied, "Hell, I don't know, a few years or so?"

She then placed the rag on the nightstand and climbed back in bed with me. "Michael, believe it or not, I was telling you the truth when you and Ms. Kitty first had sex with me. I'm— or should I say, I— was a virgin until you and that big black, long, hard dick of yours came around."

I laid back in the bed as I said to her, "Girl, stop lying."

"For real, Michael. You didn't see the blood on you after you made love to me that day?" I was looking at her, feeling all sad for her, due to her looking like she was about to cry, when she continued with, "That's why Ms. Kitty hurried up and wiped me off like she did. The bitch knew I was a virgin because I told her grimy, trifling ass later on that day, when she came and asked me why I was bleeding! She thought that you had knocked my period on!"

"Damn, Nicole, I didn't know."

By now tears were jumping off of her face as I said to her, "Come here, Ma. Let me hold you."

CHAPTER 37
TRICK DADDY!

Now my black ass was laying there holding onto Nicole while she bawled her poor lil' eyes out of her head, all while I still had the beautiful Ms. Sharon waiting on my arrival.

After a few minutes of me holding and caressing Nicole, I had to finally break down and say to her, "Excuse me, beautiful, I have to be somewhere and I'm already late."

She lazily eased off of my chest and mumbled, "I know, Michael. Go ahead and handle your business. I'll be here when you get back."

I abruptly jumped out of bed headed to the bathroom so that I could take another shower before I got to Sharon's house. While Nicole lay there in bed thinking to herself, I was able to gather my thoughts and somehow figure out how I was going to juggle her feelings along with Sharon's and still be able to convince myself that Rhynyia was who I really wanted to be with.

Twenty minutes later I stepped out of the shower and sprayed on a thick layer of my Burberry cologne, so that Sharon wouldn't smell the scent of another woman on my body. I then slid on a nice pair of my tailored-made brown slacks along with a light brown long sleeve silk shirt, with a pair of dark brown Stacey Adams.

I had just walked out of my closet as Nicole yiped, "Damn, Michael, do you have to look that nice to go handle some business?"

I took a quick look into the mirror as I replied, "Girl, this lil' outfit is nothing compared to half of the Sergio Valentine suits off inside of my closet."

"Whatever, Michael. You look like you're about to go to one of our shows without us."

"Never that, baby girl. I just make sure that I'm always looking my best at all times. I'll see you in a little while, okay?"

"Yes, Michael. I shall be right here waiting on your return," she gabbed as I placed my money clip into my pocket and darted downstairs to the garage.

Once inside I had to make a choice between which automobile I would be driving over to Sharon's humble abode. After about two minutes of me standing there debating, I chose the silver Infinity Q-45. I hadn't drove it but a few times after purchasing it, so I figured that I would change up in case those nosey ass detectives were following me.

I jumped on the highway headed towards Sharon's house doing about ninety miles an hour, since I was already two hours late. I had that Q-45 flying down I-4 with my sunroof wide open, jamming to some Trick Daddy. I think the song was *10-20 Life*. At that moment I was thinking of how I wished that I could have kept right on driving until I reached Daytona Beach. I shook that notion off as I realized that I had more important things to tend to.

I then got off at the downtown exit so that I could take a shortcut to her house. Traffic in Orlando was always slow during that time of the day, so I ran through the first traffic light as if I didn't have three warrants on my black ass nor any fucking driver's license. I pulled up at the next traffic light still jamming to some Trick Daddy while bouncing my head to the music at the same time when this fine-looking female pulled up next to me at the light.

CHAPTER 38
I WAS RESPONSIBLE!

I quickly stuck my head out of the window while sliding my Gucci shades down the bridge of my nose and yelled out to her, "Excuse me!"

She was sitting there at the light looking so gorgeous and fine in her red Mercedes Benz, when she replied. "Yes, can I help you?" she asked me while showing me all her white, nice veneers in her mouth.

"Nice car! Does your husband wash it every day?"

She continued smiling as she replied. "I'm not married, if that's what you're trying to insinuate on the sly tip!"

Bingo! Just what I wanted to hear as you know what took place next. I had her pull over at the 7-Eleven that was down the road from the light on the left-hand side of the road. Just as soon as I got the digits, she was off to wherever it was she had to be, while I went inside to purchase myself a Slurpee.

As I somberly drifted towards the counter to pay for the cold, refreshing beverage, I was musing over poor Sharon and trying to imagine what she was going through. Her cousin was dead, now here it was that her uncle was missing, and she was calling me for comfort and support. All I could think of was what I was going to say to her that would help her ease the pain of her loss.

As I pulled up in her driveway, it was cars everywhere. I could barely find me a spot to park as I nudged the Infinity up towards the entrance of her driveway. I got out of my car, headed to her front door when I spotted this beautiful, older-looking woman standing off to the side of the house, looking as if she was crying. She stood around 5'9" and weighing about a 140 pounds. She had a very nice light skin complexion with a splendid looking body. At first sight she, in some strange way, bore the striking resemblance to Rhynyia— Sexy Redd. But that notion was quickly negated from my thought pattern as I stood there stuck watching her for a brief minute or two. I knew that I was at Sharon's home, so the lovely lady had to be one of her relatives.

That's when I politely said to her, "Excuse me, ma'am?"

She lingeringly turned to face me and replied, "Yes, can I help you, young man?" She tried to smile but the pain that she held from within wouldn't let her face even think of the awful thing.

"Is Sharon in?" I asked her as I was— for the first time in my life— nervous as I approached the charming looking female.

"Oh, you must be Michael!" she asked me while catching me by surprise as she uttered my name from her splendid looking lips that I wanted to take into my mouth at the sight of seeing them. "I'm Sharon's mother. Nice to finally meet you," she said to me while she held out her arms to embrace me.

"The pleasure is all mine, ma'am," I replied as we both hugged one other.

Damn, now just seeing this beautiful creature of a woman, I knew exactly where Sharon had got her good looks from. But as I our bodies embraced, it felt faintly similar to another person's embrace.

Naw, it can't be, I said to myself as I backed away gazing at how lovely she looked. I could see in her eyes that she had been crying as I said to her, "I'm sure that everything will be okay, ma'am."

She stood there for a brief minute and then uttered, "Yes, I certainly hope so. This family can only take so much. By the way, my name is Karen, and once again it's nice to finally meet the man who is responsible for all of this!"

I was dumbfounded when she hit me with that. Did she really know that I was the person responsible for all the pain that her family was going through?

CHAPTER 39
MY COUSIN TAMEKIA!

I was standing there asking myself if she somehow knew that I had took out her niece and was the man responsible for giving the green light on her thirsty ass half-brother Fats, who was considered her baby brother? It seemed that they had the same father but different mothers.

"Excuse me ma'am?" I asked her with a shocked tone in my voice.

"Without your help, Michael, I don't know how this family would have made it this far."

For a minute there I thought that she had figured my black ass out. That's when I had realized that I told Sharon I would help pay for the burial of her cousin. I looked into her mother's eyes and muttered, "Don't mention it, Ms. Karen. I felt somewhat obligated to help with the funeral at a time like this."

She gave me a warm half-smile and then put her head down as she continued to walk alone.

At that moment things were so fucked up as I grayly walked inside the house. Her aunts, uncles and cousins were all gathered around, talking amongst one another as I walked throughout the house speaking and acknowledging the different people in attendance; when I saw Sharon standing in her kitchen talking with some female who had her back towards me. I couldn't see her face until I got inside of the kitchen. When I finally got close enough to Sharon, she reached out for me to hug her.

With her eyes being partially still watered, she softly said to me, "Baby, you finally made it."

A simple shy smile broke out on her face. I already had her body submerged in my arms as my nose caught a smell of an aroma that I had smelled a many times before. It was a fragrance that Sexy Redd used to always wear.

How was it that Sharon enjoyed the same fragrance as

Sexy Redd, I asked myself as I stood there smiling at her, when I looked up to see who the female was that she was in the kitchen talking to.

The young lady looked very familiar, as if she was someone that I knew from my past. "My God," is what I uttered under my breath while looking at this woman, who looked as she remembered my face also.

Sharon and I released the grip from one another as she introduced me to her cousin. "Michael, this is my cousin Tamekia."

"Hi, nice to meet you," I said as I held out my hand to greet her.

"And Tamekia, this is Mr. Michael Vallentino."

She then placed a familiar smile on her face and replied, "Same here, Mr. Michael. I finally get to meet the man who my dear cousin talks about all the time." She continued smiling at me.

"Naw, not poor ole me," I said back to her while blushing. I was definitely caught off guard as this beautiful, gorgeous looking female kept talking to Sharon and me. I had leaned back up against the counter with my arms folded, saying to myself, *I know her fine ass from somewhere, I just can't picture it right now!*

Sharon then brought me back from where my mind had drifted off to with, "Bae, do you want something to drink?"

I looked down at her sexy ass and replied with a smile covering my greasy ass face, "Yes boo, do you have any orange juice?"

"Orange juice coming right up, sir," she said to me as she opened the fridge to get me the cold juice.

I then turned back around to see Tamika standing behind me as if she wanted to continue talking with me.

CHAPTER 40
FROM MY PAST!

I couldn't help but stand there and stare at how fine and po-
etic her cousin looked, with me uttering to myself, *Damn, is
everybody in Sharon's family fine like this?*

Sharon then handed me the glass of Juice. "Here you go,
baby."

"Thank you, boo." I grabbed the glass of juice from her
hand and took the first sip.

I was standing directly behind Sharon when I guess the
one lady who was Do-Dirty's mother stood up and said to
everyone, "I would like to thank you all for coming out today at the last minute. As you all know, my youngest daughter was found murdered and burned to death at the paper
mill, with some of her friends. The police claim they don't
have any leads at this time. Now, earlier this morning, we
find out that Bernard 'Fats' Walker, who was my brother is
missing. And the circumstances lead to foul play."

As she continued talking I kept sipping and thinking, *If
y'all knew what I did, you all would give up any hope on
finding the person or persons responsible for her untimely
demise or his unexpected disappearance.*

Then her mother went on to say, "The funeral is this
Saturday at eleven o'clock at Agape Assembly Baptist
Church, downtown by the arena. The Reverend presiding
over her home going service is none other than the well-
renowned Reverend Travis Elrod Johebus Gallon."

Everyone turned around looking at one another when
she said his name.

I bent my head down and asked Sharon, "Why is everyone whispering amongst one another about that particular
Pastor?"

She swiftly turned her head around with a surprised look
on her face, and asked me, "Michael, shut your mouth. You
mean to tell me that you don't know who Pastor Travis

Elrod Johebus Gallon is?"

I just shrugged my shoulders as I looked at her and replied, "Naw. Why am I supposed to know who in the hell he is?"

"Boy, stop. He is one of the most expensive ass preachers here in Orlando. Thank God that you said that you would help pay for the funeral!" she said as she placed a smirk on her face and turned her head around to witness the same thing I was seeing.

I began choking as the female who I had met at the light, walked out from one of the back rooms.

She saw me standing behind Sharon and cut a shy half grin in my direction, as she walked into the living room and sat right dab smack next to Sharon's beautiful mother.

Sharon then turned her head around again and looked up at me and said, "That's my mother's baby sister. Have you met her yet?"

While gulping down the remainder of my juice that I had in my glass, I looked down at her short, fine ass and sputtered my sentiments under my breath. "Yeah, I met her. Yes, I most certainly have met her!" I was amazed that the world was that small.

In just the few hours of me being at the house, I'd met her mother's baby sister, and some female from my past that I was pretty sure would be revealed before I left that day. Could my luck get any worse than it already was? I didn't know, but I was about to quickly find out.

CHAPTER 41
CASH AND FOOD ASSISTANCE!

Do-Dirty's mother was still talking as I stood there with my mouth wide open, with the fact that I had just met the woman who sat by Sharon's mom at the red light and obtained her phone number as well. Sharon was still standing in front of me smiling at her aunt, while pointing back at me; letting her know that I was the man she had been telling her entire family about. I was standing there with the dumbest look on my face that I had ever had, hoping, and praying that her aunt wouldn't tell her about our little secret.

"We're all going to meet here at Sharon's house and then leave from here, headed to the church. After we finish eating at the church the immediate family will be returning back here to eat with the family," her aunt said, as she paused for a minute and then wiped away a single tear from her left eye. I was still somewhat in a daze as I heard Sharon's aunt say to the crowd of people who had assembled at Sharon's house, "I would like to thank Mr. Michael Vallentino here for helping the family with the burial of my baby girl. Without him, her funeral would not be taking place!" She then stood firm as one of her sisters stood next to her, holding her up, while the tears raced down her face.

She then began ushering the heavy-set woman down next to her, while I said to myself, *Damn, I know that's right!* Everybody was sitting there looking at me while I was standing there nervous as fuck! If they only knew what I knew they wouldn't be thanking me; they would all be trying to kill my ass!

Sharon and I were still standing in the kitchen area with our arms wrapped around one another, when one of her female cousins jumped up and yelled, "I know him from somewhere!"

Aww shit, I'm about to be exposed. The gig was up for poor ole Michael Vallentino.

Just like that, it's about to be curtains for me when she said it again, but louder this time. "Yeah, I know where I know him from now!"

"Where child?" another cousin shouted as if her cousin were about to reveal the winning lotto numbers to the crowded room.

"He's the man from...!" *Here it comes. Should I say my goodbye's now or just haul ass right out of the front door?*

I was still standing there without any back up at all— no Murder Queens to have my back and with Sharon's uncles and cousins blocking the door, I was cornered.

Then this lil' chicken head of a cousin finally figured out. "He used to be my case manager at the Wages Program!"

Wow, I thought that I was gone for sure. I released my ass cheeks and took a deep breath while everyone continued talking amongst themselves. I then looked at the young female and simply smiled back at her because she was absolutely right. I did have her on my caseload. But her lazy ass never came back in after her first Wages Seminar, leaving me with no other choice but to terminate her food and cash assistance.

CHAPTER 42
SOLD OUT PRINCE CONCERT

Sharon then nudged at my shirt and pulled my head down closer to her mouth, whispering in my ear, "Thank you for coming. I really need you here with me right now."

I whispered back, "I know. I need you, too." I then kissed her on her soft, tender lips.

One of her big, black ass uncles stood up and voiced, "Just to clarify a few things about our brother. The police did say that they had one clue and that it is a picture of some female Fats was seen with last before he disappeared."

"Yep, that sounds just like his Fats crazy ass. Always up in some young woman's ass! Serves his nasty, fat, black ass right. That's what his ass gets for trusting these lil' fast, hot ass girls," the lil' short fat, stocky, dark skinned woman said, as she was sitting over in the corner stuffing her face with some fried chicken, macaroni and cheese and collard greens.

Sharon looked at me and uttered, "That's his wife. Look at her fat, trifling ass, still fucking eating and we can't find my damn uncle. Chances are she probably is the one who has his ass missing."

"Damn," was all I could say as I stood there looking at how hideous this woman looked. No wonder poor Fats wanted to eat out my girl's ass the way he did. His wife looked just like a black wild hog in the face and by the darkness of her skin.

"Mom, he's still my father, so you don't have to talk about him like that. Let's just hope and pray that he's somewhere safe and sound," the tall, dark skinned young man said as he stood up, looking just like his father. He gradually slid his slender posture over by Sharon and I and said to me, "Excuse me, Mr. Vallentino."

I looked at the young man with a stern look on my face and said, "Yes, young man? Can I help you?"

He held his head down. "My father once told me that he knew you. Is there any way that you could help us locate him, sir?"

I stood firm as a gut wrenching feeling crept deep within the bowels of my stomach before saying, "Yes, if I hear of anything, I'll be sure to let the authorities and the family members know."

"Thank you, sir."

"No problem, son. You're very welcome," I said to him as he walked away with his head still down.

"Michael, I never knew that you knew of my uncle," Sharon said to me while looking amazed.

"Yeah, I met the ole boy a few times," I replied back to her while not letting her know that at one point and time he worked for me.

"Well, that was Bernard Junior, my uncle's only son." Sharon smiled, holding onto me as if I were going to make a run for the door the first moment that I saw my way out.

The family continued talking and trying to ignore Fats' wife when there was a hard knock at the door. When the one uncle who looked like he could be Fats' twin brother opened the door, you wouldn't believe who was behind it, smiling as their crooked assess came through as if they were the main attraction at a sold out Prince concert.

CHAPTER 43
YOUR TWIN BROTHER!

Detective onion head ass Protho, along with his tall, lanky ass partner detective Marty Pass slowly walked into the house with mild smirks across their faces. As they were walking and greeting people, I was busy looking for the nearest exit so I could get the hell out of there. But like I had stated earlier, Sharon's uncles were standing by the door like they were waiting for a brother to run.

That's when I quickly turned to look out of the back door so I could ease out from there. But to my surprise there were people standing out there as well. All kind of mad thoughts began to run through my mind as I looked back at Sharon and said, "Boo, do you mind if I use your bathroom please?"

She politely turned back to me and whispered, "Nah, baby, follow me." She then took me by the hand and led me down the hallway to the master bedroom.

Just as she opened the door, sat her daughter and a few of the other relatives' kids, watching cartoons. I spoke to all the kids as I numbly walked through the room. Sitting over in the corner where Do-Dirty's two lil' girls off to the side playing by themselves, with one of them looking just like my cousin Richard, while the other looked just like her mother. Damn, every room had a reminder of Do-Dirty in it as if she lived there with Sharon. I could tell that her family really loved her and how much she would be missed. I wittily gathered my thoughts and dashed for the bedroom after staring at the kids without a mother.

Upon entering the bathroom, I once again looked at my reflection in the mirror. *How could I live with myself? How could I continue facing her relatives after what I did*, I said to myself while having my head bent down over the sink. At that very moment, my world was about to change. It was as though I was deep in a trance. I couldn't believe it at first, but when I tell you what happened next, it was mind blowing and I never saw it coming.

Even though I was stressing and not getting enough sleep, I still maintained my composure and neat appearance. While still looking in the mirror, my inner person stepped out of me and began talking to me. "Listen, Michael, you have to get a grip on yourself. If not, you might as well go back out front and let those two crooked ass cops take both of our black assess to jail! Now, there are going to be times when you can't handle what's going on around you. That's when I'll step in and take care of whatever it is going on. I'll do the talking and thinking whenever times get hard for you. All you have to do is just pretend to be listening to whatever is being said at that very moment.' I was seeing double as this other me was standing right in front of me, explaining to me what was about to start taking place.

"So how long have you been with me?" I asked.

"I've been here with you since the day you were conceived, my friend," he answered.

"So, where have you been all the crucial times of my life?" I asked while feeling weak and seeming somewhat dizzy.

"I have always been here. It's now that you need me the most, so I'm here to make the tough decisions that you, for some odd reason no longer can make. In other words, Michael, I'm your conscience. Only thing different from you and others is that you will be able to see me so that you will know that I'm here for you at all times. Just think of me as your twin brother!"

CHAPTER 44
CARTOONS

I was mystified or maybe shocked as I stood there with my back propped against the wall, talking to myself. "How long will you be here with me?" I asked as I stared at my exact double.

"As long as I have to. You are more important out here than in there," he replied as he revealed an evil grin on his face.

"Where is in there?" I asked my conscience as he stood there looking me up and down as if he couldn't believe the resemblance either.

"Jail, Michael, jail. Now wash your hands and get yourself together. We have to go out here and talk with these two detectives. Besides, Sharon is about to knock on the door."

"What did you say?"

"I said that Sharon is about to knock on the door," he replied with a bit of urgency in his voice.

"How do you know that?" I asked him with an alarmed look on my face.

"Because I have what we all have but just don't use it in the right way," he replied, still showing off his evil looking grin.

"And what is that?" I asked him, but just as I had, Sharon was gently tapping on the door of the bathroom, which startled me at first but I abruptly regrouped.

"Michael, are you okay in there?"

I could hear her daughter in the background saying to her, "Mommy, he's in there talking to someone!" I was just coming from behind the door, while her daughter was standing with her mom by the door, waiting to see who I was talking to.

She pulled the door open as I walked past her drying my hands off. "Michael, were you in the bathroom with someone else?" Sharon asked me as she looked behind the door.

I gave her a quizzical look and replied, "Nah, boo. Who would I have been in the bathroom with?"

Sharon then looked down at her young daughter and said, "Baby, there is no one else in there."

Breanna looked up at her mother still looking muddled and uttered, "But I heard him talking with someone, mommy." She kept trying to convince Sharon as Sharon was kneeling down with her arms wrapped around her daughter.

I just stood there gazing at the beauty that laid there between Sharon's thighs and couldn't help but fantasize about our love escapade in which we would be caught in after all of her relatives left.

Meanwhile my conscience was standing behind me, looking directly at her daughter with his right index finger over his mouth. "Shhhh. Be quiet, my child," he whispered to Breanna.

The young child then put her head down as if she had just been scolded for being a bad girl.

He then winked at her as Sharon turned around looking at me and spoke.

"Michael, what kind of silly games are you playing with my daughter?"

She was still smiling as I came back with, "Sharon, now what would make you think something like that?"

We both walked back outside of her bedroom holding hands when I could still hear Breanna yelling to her mother. "Mommy, what about the other Mr. Michael, still back here in the room with us?"

Sharon turned back and yelled, "Baby, there is no one there; I checked. Now finish watching your cartoons!"

The other kids then all ran to the door screaming, "We heard someone in there too, auntie!"

CHAPTER 45
UNTIMELY DEMISE!

I had a unique, genuine smile across my face as we walked back into the living room, when I looked down at Sharon and voiced, "Your family is a trip."

She cut a shy gaze up at me and quickly replied, "Whatever, Michael. All I know is that you better not be trying to scare my daughter and her cousins."

"Never that, boo," I replied while feeling like I was on top of the world. I was, until we both reached the living room where everyone else was.

Just as soon as those two crooked ass cops saw my face, I heard a familiar voice yell out to me. "Excuse me, Mr. Vallentino, could we have a brief minute of your time please sir!" Detective Protho shouted.

"Excuse me, Sharon, while I go see what these two dickhead cops want."

"Do you need me to come with you, baby?" she asked while holding on tightly to my hand.

"Nah, handle your family, I'll be just a few minutes," I said to her as I patted her on the hand and walked through the crowd of people who had gathered at her place, all looking at me like I had stolen something.

The cops and I wandered outside as my conscience looked over at me and said to me with an imperiling grin on his face, "The answer to your question that you asked me earlier is that I can see things minutes before they are about to happen. Now watch and take notes in regard to the way I handle these two dumb ass cops!"

I must have blacked out and my conscience took over from there, because I never saw what took place next.

Detective Protho started the conversation off with, "Mr. Vallentino, we had a few clues as to who blew up that old paper mill off of Highway 98 and Hubert Hurst Road. That was until our main witness somehow disappeared. Then we find out that he and one of the victims were related, along with one of the other victims, who you had working for you."

"Is that so and what does this have to do with me?" my conscience uttered as he stood there cool as the devil himself.

"Because all three victims at some point of time all worked for you in some type of capacity," Detective Protho replied as he continuously sucked on a red cherry flavored lollipop.

"Yes, that they did, but I had to fire their thieving asses for trying to steal from me!"

"Funny, sir, now two of them are dead with another one fucking missing."

"Well, what do you want me to say? You know shit does happen."

"Yes, it does and for some strange reason it happens a lot around you," Detective Pass chimed in as he was looking around at all the nice cars parked in Sharon's yard.

"So what? I know you're not trying to implicate me into the equation?"

"Nah, but we did run into one thing."

"Okay and what was that?"

"It seems as though it was a limo that was seen leaving the crime scene in a hurry on the day the place went up in smoke."

"Okay."

"The limo in question seems to be registered to a company that your precious Florida Hot Girls helped finance. By the name of Prestige Limo Service."

"I see. Well, we have a few companies throughout Orlando that are financed through the Florida Hot Girls."

"Funny thing about that as well, Mr. Vallentino, is that two of the dead victims were seen that same day getting out of that particular limo. Now we can't seem to find that limo or the Jamaican driver, who witnesses say dropped them off at the local car wash across from the Caribbean Beach Night Club the day they met their untimely demise. So, do you know anything about that?"

Damn.

Michael Gallon

CHAPTER 46
NOPE, CAN'T SAY I DO

The questions and the thought of the victims running throughout my mind made my conscience reply back with. "Wow, it seems like you two guys know a lot already. I believe if you two clowns want to keep asking me any more questions, it would be in my best interest to have my attorney present with me. I don't want to say the wrong thing because we all know how the cops can misconstrue someone's words around. In other words, you won't have my black ass on the six o'clock news!"

"So, you're guilty, Mr. Vallentino?"

"Why of course not, Detective Protho."

"So tell us then, what do we do now? Since you don't seem to want to tell us what really happened to your friends."

"Who said that they were my gotdamn friends? Hell, I barely knew their asses. If you want to know anything personal about the one female named Do-Dirty and her damn uncle, just walk your JC Penney suit wearing ass inside and ask them folks!"

"Whoa, hold on there, cowboy. What's up with all the hostility?"

"C'mon detective, let's stop pulling each other's chain. You two clowns are out here asking me questions like I know what happened to them fools. I don't know and don't care."

"Okay, well help us help you. You seem as if you don't know that you have three open warrants that we could take you downtown for right now."

My conscience tensed up and then replied with. "Okay, let's not take it there. In most cases like this, the best thing to do would be to just leave well enough alone. And just make it seem like you two ran into a brick wall or something.

"So, you're trying to pay us off, Mr. Vallentino?"

"Nah, why do you say that? All I'm saying is that since your star witness has decided to leave town, maybe I can just help you guys make this case disappear."

"Sounds like your trying to bribe two law enforcement officers, sir," Detective Pass said while rubbing his greasy ass hands together.

Just then, Sharon waltzed outside saying to me. "Honey, is everything alright out here?"

I looked over at the officers and then back to Sharon who had walked up on us.

"Yeah, I think that we are all done out here, baby," I replied while placing my hands into my pants pocket.

She looked over into the faces of the two officers while smiling at the both of them and asked. "So officers, do you all have any clues to where my uncle might be or what may have happened to him?"

Detective Protho went into the pocket of his JC Penny suit, pulled out a picture and showed it to Sharon. He was licking his lips all while staring at her beauty.

"All we have is this picture of the young woman your uncle mentioned in his text. Do you know her?"

As Sharon looked down at the picture, I took a look for myself from over her shoulder to see that it was a picture of Yani with a blonde wig on her head.

"No, I can't say that I do, officer. Bae, do you know her?" Sharon asked as she looked up into my face.

"I quickly muttered back to her. "Nope, can't say I do!"

CHAPTER 47
TWO HUNDRED AND FIFTY THOUSAND

Shit had just got real for the Murder Queens and me. I stood there motionless after seeing the photo of Yani.

"Don't you all have face recognition or some type of technology that would pull her face up?" Sharon asked as she stared back at the two detectives.

"Yes, we do ma'am, but your uncle must have had a very cheap phone due to the quality of the photo. Plus, she must have seen that he was trying to snap her photo. She turned her head just in time, preventing him from snapping her picture," Detective Protho replied.

"Or maybe the young lady was a bit camera shy and didn't want her picture taken," my conscience said to the detectives as the both of them were still staring at Sharon. She was standing there in a nice sundress along with some nice ass Gucci heels on her feet. They also could see how nice her round red ass looked in her sundress due to the sun beaming down on her.

"So, I take it that you detectives don't have anything else to go by, do you?" Sharon asked as she was trying to get the two of them to look her in her eyes instead of at her body.

"Sharon, calm down, baby. I'm sure these two fine detectives are doing their best to find the criminals behind this terrible incident," my conscience replied as he placed his arms on the shoulders of Sharon.

"Yes, your right, Michael," Sharon said. "Officers please forgive me. You have to try and understand how much of a toll this is taking on me and my family right now. First, my dear cousin was found dead and burned past recognition. Now, my damn uncle is fucking missing."

"Believe me when I tell you ma'am, we do understand. As we told you earlier when we met you at Mr. Vallentino's apartment, we always get our man. Believe that!" Detective Protho sputtered as he cut his eyes over at me while grinning.

"Alright, well I'll be inside if you all need me. Do you all know how much longer it will be before Michael can join us back inside?"

"We should be done with him in the next few minutes or so ma'am," Detective Pass replied, as Sharon slowly turned and walked away.

"Ump, ump, ump, boy she sure is the definition of a beautiful black woman. If you ever get tired of her nice red ass, Michael, I would love to have her in my bed at night time!" Detective Protho voiced as he grabbed his crotch smiling as he gazed at Sharon.

I cut a wicked smile back at him and uttered. "Whatever. You don't have what it takes to pull a female like her."

"That's what your mouth says young man. Just as soon as we pin all these murders on your black ass, she will be begging for me to give her this dick," Protho replied as his partner stood there laughing at what he had just voiced.

"I thought that I was going to help you guys make this case go away."

"Yeah, if you can get us two of those big ass houses that your black ass has somehow managed to move into. Along with two of those black big body Mercedes Benz and to top it all off, we're going to need two hundred and fifty thousand dollars apiece in our bank accounts. So my partner and I can go on a nice vacation with our wives."

CHAPTER 48
MY FUTURE AND MY PAST

As Detective Protho continued telling me what they wanted as if I was the black Santa Claus of Orlando, I was standing there looking like they had just lost their muthafucking minds.

"Ah okay, so that's all that you guys want right? And then this case will just up and disappear?"

Detective Protho was nodding his head up and down as he replied with. "Yes!"

"Okay, just let me make a few phone calls. Is there a number that I can get back in touch with you guys at?"

"Yep, here it is."

I took the card and asked. "One more question, what about the families of the victims?"

"Fuck 'em. They'll just have to get over it like they do everything else in their sorry ass miserable lives!" Detective Protho replied as he grinned at me and then crunched down on his cherry flavored lollipop. Then, throwing the stick in my direction. I quickly moved out of the way of the stick as Detective Pass mumbled.

"Yeah lil' ass nigga. You just worry about getting us our fucking money, our very own nice big ass houses along with two black big body Mercedes Benz!" He then placed his hands inside of his suit pants pocket to retrieve the keys to their black police issued sedan.

Just as the two crooked cops pulled out of the driveway, I must've snapped back from out of my trance as one of the kids playing outside ran up behind me. "Hey Mr., when I grow up I want to be just like you!" He said sounding all excited.

I kneeled down to speak with the young man who couldn't have been no older than ten years old. "Now, why do you want to grow up like me?"

"Because every time I see you, you always have a

different girlfriend with you."

I smiled at the young man as I went into my pocket to give him a few dollars. Just as I had handed him a ten dollar bill, his mother walked out of the house, calling out to him.

"Lil Michael, let's go son!"

I turned around to see who his mother was. When I saw her face again, it was the woman that Sharon was talking to earlier in her kitchen.

"Damn, that's his mother," I said to myself as young Michael ran over to where she was standing. He turned back and yelled out to me. "Thank you Mr. Michael, and it was nice seeing you again!"

I was standing there in shock and disbelief trying to find something to come back with as I watched them climb into their car. They were just about to drive past me when the mother rolled down her window and muttered. "Boy, you sure get around don't you?"

"Excuse me, do I know you?" She smiled at me as she replied.

"Remember when you used to be the manager at Value Pawn on Orange Blossom Trail? Think about it. Give it about ten minutes to sink in!"

She then blew me a kiss as she drove away with her lil' son and daughter waving bye to me. I stood there for a minute or two trying to remember her face but all I could think of was her son and the cute lil' girl that sat in the backseat buckled up in the car.

Damn, not only was my future fucking with my mind, but my past was starting to catch up to me as well. *Where in the hell did I know her from?* I asked myself as I sluggishly walked back inside of Sharon's house.

CHAPTER 49
MY FIRST SON!

Before I could get in the door of the overcrowded house, Sharon's mother snatched me by the arm and started talking to me about how she had heard so much about me but had never actually met me.

As I tentatively sat there watching and listening to this woman rant, I could see a striking resemblance to Rhynyia. Her facial features along with the way she carried her hands seemed to be identical to the way Rhynyia would act whenever she was excited about telling me something, or whenever she became enraged about anything that set her off.

I sat there trying to shake that notion out of my mind as I drifted back and forth, thinking about what those two crooked ass cops wanted. The same damn thing that Sharon's mother baby brother wanted. And then there was the female who had just left, talking about we used to be more than friends. It was entirely too much for me to take in. I needed to somehow get out of that house and away from all those people before my fucking head exploded.

Just as I moved to one spot to the next, someone was pulling at me by my shirt so that they could talk to me. As I looked down at my watch, it was already somewhere around eight thirty p.m. My entire day had been taken away from me and I hadn't been able to spend at least thirty minutes alone with Sharon's fine ass. I knew that she was going to want me to spend the night or her to spend the night back at my place.

My environment was starting to become really complicated, with no sign of help nowhere in sight. I was sitting there looking around as question after question was being asked of me. I saw my conscience sitting across from me with his legs crossed, looking like he could've been the devil himself.

With all the noise and commotion going on throughout

the house, I couldn't hear any of it as my conscience spoke to me. "Okay, just calm down and get a grip on yourself. Now look around at your surroundings. Take a very deep breath and continue to look around. There is nothing to concern yourself with but what's ahead of you right now. Those two cops, we need to take them out just like we did everybody else!"

"No, no more killing. We have done too much of that for now!" I sharply said back to my conscience as beads of sweat rolled down my forehead.

He slid off of the couch as he spat back at me with. "Exactly my man. We have done too much to turn around and we haven't done enough to just stop. We have to keep going before they start to want a part of what we both love the most."

"And what is that?" I asked.

"You know what," he angrily replied.

"No!" I yelled back to my conscience before he stood up and shouted back at me.

"Yes, the Florida Hot Girls."

"No!" I spoke as I jumped up into his face screaming out loud.

The entire room got quiet as I was looking around at everyone who sat there shocked looking back at me.

Sharon being quick minded, ran over to me and said. "Michael, what's wrong? You must have fell asleep and had a very bad dream. Come on baby, follow me to my bedroom. Excuse me everyone while I make sure he's alright," Sharon said to the crowd of people as she placed her arm around my waist and whisked my crazy ass back to her bedroom.

I was stumbling and walking as if I was in a daze as she walked me down the hallway. She looked up at me. "Baby, you really need to get some rest. Have you been taking your medication that the doctor prescribed for you?"

I ponderously replied. "No, I didn't think that I needed

it anymore."

She sat me on the edge of her bed and took off my Stacey Adams. She looked up at me with her nice hazel brown eyes. "Michael, baby you have to take your pills. Lord only knows what I would do without you here to help me raise our son."

I was stunned or maybe shocked as I looked down at her and said, "Our son?"

She looked back at me with a single tear streaming down her right cheek. "Yes, Michael, I'm having your son."

I sat there with a lonely tear running down my face as the thought of this beautiful woman having my first son set in.

Michael Gallon

CHAPTER 50
BACK IN MY STOMACH

The very next day was business as usual. I had stayed the night at Sharon's house, so I didn't know what to expect when I got back home. I had been put through a very long and vigorous night with Sharon. You see as soon as all her family members had left, she gave her daughter a quick bath and then tore off into my black ass.

As I laid there half sleep dreaming of better times, she rolled my ass over and took care of herself before I could even get me. She fell off of me quickly and plummeted into a very deep sleep. I guess she was tired from the long hard day that she had with her family members.

Now that I was back home, the first person I ran into was Entyce. She was at the pool with her newfound friend by the name of Reese. She had met the young man one night at one of our shows and ever since that night, she was feeling him as he was somewhat feeling her.

Now Reese was an ex-member of the world famous rap group called The 69 Boyz. He had told Entyce that he was one of the dancers in the group. But you know me, I never saw his ass on stage whenever they were performing. Who knows? Maybe he had been fired before I saw them.

The guy had nowhere to stay so Entyce wanted him staying with us. At first, things were okay until she started seeing little signs of more than what Reese was telling her.

After seeing the both of them at the pool area, acting as if they were the only ones around, I jogged upstairs to find the other females all inside of Mignon's room chit chatting and just hanging out.

Nicole yelled out to me. "Damn, that pussy must have been all that since you couldn't come home last night, playa!"

I peeked my head through the door and replied back with. "Not as good as yours, beautiful."

She started screaming and yelling as she ran over to me and gave me a nice size hug and kiss in front of the other females inside of Mignon's bedroom. "I'm glad that your home, daddy. I missed you last night!"

"Nicole, please, you didn't miss me."

"Yes I did, I missed you and this dick." She grabbed me by my manhood while the other girls were sitting there looking at us interacting with one another.

"I can't wait until your back inside of my stomach, Michael," Nicole said out loud so that the other women could hear what she had said to me.

"So you're going to eat his dick off of the bone too, Nicole?" Strawberry said as the girls all burst into laughter.

"Man you women are a trip. Do you all have everything ready for tonight's show?" I asked them as they all looked around at each other with smiles on their bright faces.

"Oh yeah, we do have Apollo South and Hollywood Nites tonight," Mignon said while standing up off of her bed with her nice ass camel toe protruding out of her tight ass boy shorts.

"Damn Mignon, please put away all of that phat ass kitty kat of yours back in your shorts!" I yelled in excitement.

"Whatever, Mike. You probably want some of it, anyway, don't you?" She said with a smile on her face as Nicole stood there waiting for me to answer.

"Nah Mignon, I have enough kitty kat all around me at all times."

"I know that's right," Nicole said to Mignon as she followed me into my bedroom.

I was inside my closet looking for an outfit when Nicole climbed up into my bed and crossed her legs Indian style. "So Sharon had you all tied up last night I see?"

"Nah, it got late so I decided to stay over at her place. You don't mind, do you?"

Nicole looked up at me with a disarming smile and then uttered, "Whatever, Michael. I was worried about your sexy

118

black ass."

"Well why didn't you call me to make sure that I was good?"

"Because I knew that you were with your baby mamma, and I didn't want to interrupt you while you were with her. I have to respect her even if I do want her man all to myself."

Michael Gallon

CHAPTER 51
MICHAEL AND I

Nicole stated to me as she sat there on my bed with her legs crossed. I densely turned back towards her and replied, "Thank you for understanding."

I walked up on her so that she could see the concern in my face as I spoke with her. I sat on the edge of the bed and said, "Listen, I thought I would never have to tell you this, but I have a job for you and your friends called the Murder Queens."

"Now that's what the fuck I'm talking about!" she said to me as she jumped off of the bed, looking at me while rubbing her hands together and smiling at me with anticipation on what I had to say. "Excuse me real quick, Michael." She blurted out as she ran down the hallway screaming. "Hey ladies, Michael needs to speak with all of us real quick. Strawberry go get Entyce!"

Minutes later, every one of the females that resided with me were inside my room sitting on my bed as I stood over by the window explaining to them what needed to be done. It took me about forty minutes to explain to them what needed to take place without a hitch. I glanced down at my time piece and then back up at them with. "Alright, now that we have that out of the way, let me get some rest before we have to leave for the show tonight. Nicole, please check on the ladies that are riding with us and wake me up around six o'clock this evening."

"Yes, Michael, do you want anything to eat before you take a nap?"

"Not right now, Nicole. I'm going to try to get me some needed rest right now. Maybe I'll have a sandwich or something when I wake up."

I was so tired that I was asleep before my head hit the pillow. I laid there dreaming of the day when I would finally see my Princess Sexy Redd once again.

***

Meanwhile, back in her native homeland, Puerto Rico, Rhynyia and her father, Pierre Santiago were walking through her stepmother's Botanical Garden talking to one another. While admiring all the beautiful plants that adorned her garden, her father had his arms behind his back as the both of them walked and discussed old times. He lethargically looked over at the lovely looking Rhynyia and said, "So, my elegant first born child, how was your stay in beautiful Orlando, Florida?"

While waiting for her response, he plucked a red rose and placed it in her beautiful long black hair.

"It was beautiful father. How I wish that you could have come to visit me there, at least one time. Maybe then you and I could have searched for my mother together."

"Yes, that could have been an adventure all within itself. Did you have any luck in finding your gorgeous mother?" Pierre asked as he turned his head looking directly into his daughter's eyes.

"Not at all fathers. It was one dead end after another one. Michael used to work for a program that helped women on welfare find employment. He told me that he would use his contacts to help locate her for me," Rhynyia answered sounding so sure that I would find her mother.

"This Michael seems to be like a very reliable asset to whatever your needs seem to be, my dear."

"Yes father and that is the way that I would like to keep it," Rhynyia said as she stared her father directly back in his face.

"Rhynyia, why do you say it like that my dear? As if I'm going to do something wrong to this man that I've never met! "

"Because father, I know that you only deal with men if they can help you in return."

Her father looked back at her and answered, "Rhynyia

that is the way that you should always conduct yourself when it comes to doing business with someone."

"But father, you don't have any business with Michael!"

"Yes, that is correct, but I will when he arrives to the island next week," Pierre said with a wicked smile on his face.

Rhynyia quickly stopped walking as she stared her father deeply into his dark eyes. "Listen father, Michael is more than just my boyfriend and the man I love. He's the man that I want to spend the rest of my life with."

Pierre smiled as he said, "Do I hear wedding bells in the air, my dear?"

Rhynyia began to smile as Pierre looked at his daughter who had matured into the exact replica of her elegant, gorgeous looking mother. She blushed as her father continued to look upon her beauty.

She then broke her smile as she said, "Father, there is something that I must tell you about Michael and I.

Michael Gallon

PART 3
CHAPTER 52
I'M WITH CHILD

Pierre paused for a second and spoke. "Yes, my child, it seems as though you have already told me a great deal about you and this man called Michael Vallentino." He picked up a stone and threw it into the ocean.

"Michael is the father of my unborn child."

Pierre stood frozen in his tracks for a few seconds as he abruptly turned back to Rhynyia with a look of joy in his eyes. "So, Rhynyia, you're telling me that I'm about to be a proud grandfather?"

Rhynyia raised her head as she looked her father in his eyes and replied, "Yes father, I'm with child!"

*****

Meanwhile, back in Orlando, Nicole was just entering into my bedroom to wake me up. "Michael, it's six o'clock."

I was just turning over and replied, "Thank you, Nicole." I rolled over in my bed debating on what I should wear to the club that night. I must've laid there for about thirty minutes before I finally got up and jumped into the shower. It would only be a few more hours before I would have to drive to each one of the ladies house to pick them up for the drive down to Tampa that night.

Richard would be at Apollo South with team B, while I would be inside Hollywood Nites with my beautiful amazing looking women known as team A. The girls that Richard had with him were a mixture of some of the old girls along with a few of the new ones. I would have more of the original crew of girls along with this one new chick from Eatonville by the name of Channel.

Channel stood around five foot five and weighing somewhere between one hundred and twenty five pounds to one hundred and thirty. She had a beautiful attractive smile along with a nice phat ass body that would cause many of men to want her upon seeing her walk into any club. Her chest was a nice mouthwatering thirty six B with a nice phat stupid ass that stood out on her nice brown skin complexion. It made her the complete example of what a true Florida Hot Girl should look like.

There was only one problem with this elegant looking exotic vixen. And that problem was her foul ass mouth, in which she was always challenging my authority. Because of Channel, I had to always come up with a new rule when it came to the women in my group. You see Channel had a real raspy ass voice, like Weezy Jefferson from the hit show, The Jeffersons. Her voice just drove you mad when hearing it. The later it became in the night, the worse her voice became.

What started it all was whenever we would be coming home from the club or bachelor party, Channel would have to get on her damn cell phone and start talking with whomever she could call at three something in the morning. I could hear her entire conversation from the backseat to all the way in the front seat where I would be driving everyone back home. Her voice just drove me crazy right along with any female who was trying to get some sleep. The only reason that any of the other girls wouldn't say anything to her was that they were afraid of her fighting skills as well as the skills that Chyna had.

So I had to implement the rule that no one could talk on their phones until I stopped for gas. Now while I was outside of my vehicle, you could talk to whoever it was you needed to talk to. But just as soon as I got back inside of that vehicle, all phones would have to be turned off. I didn't care if it was your damn mother that you were talking to. Whoever it was, you had to end the phone conversation right then. If I caught you breaking this rule, all hell would break lose. The first fine would be twenty five dollars at first and then go up if I caught you again that same night. Some of the girls would actually tell on one another so I would give them half of the fine money if they snitched the other one out. Now if you refused to pay the fine, you couldn't come back to work until you paid it off. Eventually, the girls made so much money some nights that they would just pay the fine first so they could talk on their phones.

I had so many females between Richard and I that I had to institute new rules on the group almost every day so that I could get rid of all the extra unwanted weight that I was carrying around.

Michael Gallon

CHAPTER 53
THAT MUCH POWER

We arrived at Apollo South around eleven fifteen that night, which gave me just enough time to walk Richard and his crew of women inside of the club.

Just to make the crowd mad, I took along a few of the girls from team A so that they could see just how many females I had with me.

After about ten minutes of me talking with the house DJ Don Juan and a few of the local females from the club who wanted to join the group, it was time for me to leave.

A few of the club patrons saw me leaving with the crew of women and started shouting in the background. "Hey man, those chicks ain't dancing in here tonight?"

I quickly turned around to whomever the voice belonged to with. "Nah my brother, they're going over to the other club with me."

"Man fuck that, we're following you to wherever them females are going!" The tall slender brother said to his table of homies that seemed to have to come to the club just to see the Florida Hot Girls.

The girls and I quickly sprinted outside and shot right over to Hollywood Nites. When we got there, the crowd was just starting to get inside. The guy who talked me into bringing my stable of ladies to his club walked up to me.

"Yo Mike, I see that you and those beautiful fine ass ladies of yours made it," he said to me as he stood there looking at all the gorgeous women that I had with me. He was grabbing his crotch as if he was about to fuck something.

"Yes I did, my brother. I told you that we were coming. Once I give a person my word, that's my promise to you. Like Tony Montana said, my word is like my balls and I don't break them for anyone or any reason," I replied as the

girls continued getting out of the truck one by one and looking like a million dollars as they all stood there waiting on
me to give them the okay to walk into the club.

The manager walked us inside the club as I heard a hater
from the standing room line that was wrapped around the
club.

"Man it don't make no sense for a brother to have them
many women who only moves when his smooth ass com-
mands them too!"

His friend, who was standing next to his short ass,
chimed in with. "Tell me about it. It makes no sense for one
brother to have that much power and he probably doesn't
have to even pay them if he wants to have his way with any
of them bad ass females."

His partner turned back to him and uttered. "Man get off
of his dick!"

"Hell you were on it before I was nigga. Just shut the
fuck up and pay our way in nigga!"

I smiled as I heard the two clowns go back and forth
amongst one another.

The manager looked up at me once the girls and I were
inside and asked me. "So Mike, how many girls do you have
with you?

"I think around twelve," I replied still smiling at my
beautiful flock of women.

"Twelve!" he said with a great big smile covering his
small face.

"Yep, twelve. Hell, I dropped another twelve off at
Apollo South. They're going to be here if they don't make
any money over there."

"Boy you're doing big things. When I grow up I want to
be just like you."

We both smiled at one another and shook hands as my
girls went straight to their dressing room and started dressing.

CHAPTER 54
SOCIAL SECURITY CHECK

As soon as the girls were all inside getting dressed, in came the hate from the other females that were inside of the club. I could hear a few of them whispering to one another as I sat down at the bar waiting on my ladies to all come out.

"Yeah, girl that's him. The guy who thinks that he's a pimp because he has all of them dumb ass broads working for his black ass!" The one short black thick ass female uttered to her friend as they stood near the rear of the club jocking me.

Truth be told is that people always hate what they don't understand. Basically, the females were hating on the girls and I because they either wanted to be in the group or they wanted to know how I had all those gorgeous females on my team. Before it was all over, the majority of them same lame ass females who hated on my crew and I that very first night, would end up dancing for me or dancing at one of my shows during my illustrious career.

At first, I felt some type of way about the reception that we received that very first night dancing at Hollywood Nites. I mean my girls had to change in the female restroom. I would have least thought that the club would have treated my ladies with a little bit more of professionalism than they did.

After thirty minutes of them dressing in, they assured me that they were all comfortable and that they would be okay. When they all came out, they were all looking fly as hell and ready to make their bread. But the most important thing of all was to let the people in Tampa, Florida know just how the females from Orlando, Florida put it down!

The crowd was becoming larger with my ladies ready to take on whatever was ahead for them that particular night.

As they all walked by me and dropped their individual bags off to me at the bar, I had begun to feel a bit more comfortable while watching all of them and saying to my-self. "Boy I hope that I haven't made the worst mistake of my life by bringing my ladies here."

After about an hour off into the club, things were flow-ing for the girls and I. Carmen and Mignon were off to the left of the club with a pile of ones at their feet. They kept right on dancing as the guys that they were dancing for kept throwing money at both of them.

Entyce and Nicole were off in the back of the club with drinks in one hand with their large Crown Royal bags off in their other hand filled to the top with dead presidents. Ni-cole seductively winked her right eye at me to let me know that she had her eyes on me. I smoothly smiled back at her as I caught Strawberry and Charlie B behind me at the bar changing in their ones. I would've never seen her if she hadn't been trying to get my attention so that I could see all the ones she had.

Meanwhile, lil' fast ass Kitty was dancing in front of me with some dude who was in a wheel chair. She was taking all the poor guys money as she looked up at me smiling.

"Damn lil' Kitty, let the poor man take home at least some of his Social Security check!" I yelled to her while looking at the large amount of money she had nestled be-tween her thin ass legs.

"Hell naw. He might as well put my name on his check because every time that I come down here his ass belongs to me!" She yelled back to me as she put her lil' small ass booty off in his face so that he could smell what she had ate only two hours earlier.

CHAPTER 55
TURNING ON ME IN THE END

My girl Chyna had her nice soft, voluptuous, big ass titties so deep off inside of this one guys face that all he could see was those nice ass titties of hers staring directly into his eyes.

I sat there with the long face as I longed for the day that I could one day have been as lucky as he was that night.

Meanwhile, JK and her girls were dancing on some guys along the rear wall of the club. As I approached them and got a better look at the guys that they were dancing on, it looked as if they could have played football for the Bucs with all the money they had between them that night. I nodded my head at them and continued to search throughout the club for my ladies.

I had just made my way back to the bar area when Suga Bear and Shortie walked by me headed to the girls' restroom. Shortie was so excited about how much money she had made in just the short time that we had been there that she neglected to do one thing. She didn't change in her ones at the bar. Her bag was so full that he could barely close it as her and her best friend staggered into the ladies room. Now, her second problem was that she had too much to drink and was still slowly drinking, when she sat her lil' drunk ass down on the toilet seat.

Her third problem was that she sat her quite large money bag down on the floor while she took a piss.

When her and Suga Bear walked back outside of the restroom laughing and playing with one another, I called out to her. "Hey Shortie, where is your damn money bag?" I asked her as her smile turned into a frown as her and Suga Bear ran back into the restroom trying to retrieve her money bag.

She yanked the door open as I could hear her scream. "Oh shit, Suga Bear, my money bag is gone.''

"Yep that is exactly what happens when you leave your money bag on the floor of a strip club. Somebody is going to pick it up every time."

Lil Shortie was devastated. She ran back throughout the club looking for her money bag screaming as if the person who took it was actually going to return it.

First of all, I didn't know of anyone ever returning a money bag to someone in the club. That lil' purple bag full of Shortie's hard earned cash was gone. She had made the awful mistake of letting that bag out of her sight. That was something that a female stripper should never do inside of a busy filled to capacity strip club.

Years later as I think back to that dreadful night Shortie lost her bag, it never dawned on me that no one went back inside of that rest room that night between the time her and Suga Bear had left. There was only one person that went in and came out, which only means one thing. Nahhhh, Suga Bear would've never stole money from one of her best friends. Believe that if you want too because in the stripping game, no one is your friend. I would learn that the hard way some thirteen years later, when the ones who I trusted the most ended up turning on me in the end.

CHAPTER 56
BERNIE MAC

The rest of the night at Hollywood Nites went well for it being the first night there for my girls and I. The crowd was nice, and the money kept flowing and besides the club had beautiful women inside it as well.

It was just a sad first night for my girl Shortie, who had lost her money bag, for being thoughtless and most of all careless. The night was the first night of a many more nights that the Florida Hot Girls would be dancing at Hollywood Nites.

Apollo South had closed around two a.m., and my cousin, Richard had already texted me to let me know that the club was slow and that his crew of extraordinary women wanted to come join me and team A at Hollywood Nites.

I gave him the approval and they all showed up around one fifteen mad and pissed off. The first female to start complaining to me was this cute bright skinned female named Angel. She was all upset and speaking for the rest of his crew of females. They all caught me at the bar with a big ass smile on my face.

"Mike, we don't ever want to go back to that club again. There is no money there and besides the crowd followed you guys over here."

She was right. In just that one night, the crowd had shifted towards Hollywood Nites and by the looks of things, that's how it was going to be from that night to this very day.

As I sat there listening to Angel complain about Apollo that early Wednesday morning, I started to realize what the guy from Hollywood Nites had said to me when he first enticed me to bring my ladies to his club.

"The crowd here in Tampa seems to follow wherever you take the Florida Hot Girls!"

He was absolutely right. After that night, Apollo South

would eventually close its doors to girls dancing there on Tuesday nights all because of me and the Hot Girls taking our show to another club.

Years later, I would regret ever changing up on Apollo South like I did. For it was Apollo South that gave the Florida Hot Girls their big break in the stripping industry. And now here it was me changing up venues. It caused one of Tampa's most prized establishments to close its doors to the stripping business. In other words, the Florida Hot Girls were responsible for one club falling and another one rising to the top.

What's more a tragic is that to this very day, time and moment, Hollywood Nites never gave me nor my stable of exotic women credit for turning their club into one of Florida's hottest night spots.

Richard and I sat there at the bar as we gazed at the gorgeous array of fabulous women we had between the both of us. Suga Bear came from the picture booth hand in hand with her new found friend who looked like some famous comedian. She caught me by surprise as she yelled out to me. "Hey Mike, look who I met!" She had a great big Kool-Aid smile across her fat wide face as Richard and I slowly turned to see what all the commotion was about.

"What the fuck?" is what I said as she just stood there beaming with joy.

"Mike here is my bar fee and fine for leaving the club. I'm going to leave with my friend, Buster."

And that is exactly what he looked like, a busted ass version of Bernie Mac on crack.

She would go on later to tell me that Buster had some real long money and that's why she fell head over heels in love with his deep chocolate looking ass.

CHAPTER 57
THE FLORIDA HOT GIRLS

Richard was so damn drunk and high when Suga Bear turned to walk away. He leaned over to me and asked me, "Hey Mike, was that really Bernie Mac old girl was with?"

I leaned back over to his square headed ass and replied, "Richard are you fucking drunk or have you been smoking with Chief smoking head ass Chazz again?"

"Nah cuz, I'm just a lil' tipsy from a few drinks that I had over at the other club. I had to drink something to help me ease the pain from me losing my kids mother," he said to me while I just sat back and thought to myself. *"Did he really love her that much and did he have any idea of what her and her trifling ass friends had planned for me?"*

Tears began to form in the well of his eyes as he turned towards me and said, "Cuz, I know that Tonya Do-Dirty wasn't the most honest chick in the world, but she was the mother of my two kids. Did you know that her and Jasmine were planning on robbing some nigga who they said had a safe and mad cash up inside of his house?"

I was really thinking to myself now as to did he actually know who they were going to rob, when his drunk ass blurted out that statement. I was just about to burst with emotions myself as he continued.

"She had such a big mouth that she told me the night before she died that her uncle had told her and Jasmine about how much money that the nigga would have stored inside of his safe."

My heart stared racing fast as I looked him squarely off in his face and asked him. "Did she tell you who it was that they were going to hit?"

"No, that she didn't tell me, but I'm pretty sure that her uncle knows who the damn nigga is. And I'm pretty sure that whoever the guy was is probably the same guy who had her and her friends killed," he stated as he gulped down the last bit of his drink.

I turned in my chair as I said to the bartender. "Excuse me, let me have something to drink please."

Richard turned to me and uttered, "Cuz, I didn't know that you drink."

"I usually don't but this morning I need one to help ease my mind as well, Richard."

"What will you be having sir?" The lovely bartender asked me as I fumbled around inside of my pocket for some loose change. I looked up at her once I found some loose dollar bills when she looked back at me and smiled. "All drinks are free for you, Mr. Vallentino.

I gently smiled back at her and replied. "Well, how about that. Okay, I'll have a Sex on The Beach please."

Richard stood up and began walking towards the men's restroom when he looked back at me and said. "Order me one too, cousin."

"Make that two please, ma'am!"

"No problem sir, right away." She turned to make the drinks as I sat there still, frozen. Thinking to myself about how I had took the life of my cousin's baby's mother, and what would Richard think once he found out that the man who actually killed his baby mother was me. And that her uncle was dead as well?

What was I becoming and what lay ahead for me and the beautiful women I had assembled known as The Florida Hot Girls?

To Be Continued...
The Murder Queens 4
Coming Soon

Lock Down Publications and Ca$h Presents assisted publishing packages.

BASIC PACKAGE $499
Editing
Cover Design
Formatting

UPGRADED PACKAGE $800
Typing
Editing
Cover Design
Formatting

ADVANCE PACKAGE $1,200
Typing
Editing
Cover Design
Formatting
Copyright registration
Proofreading
Upload book to Amazon

LDP SUPREME PACKAGE $1,500
Typing
Editing
Cover Design
Formatting
Copyright registration
Proofreading
Set up Amazon account
Upload book to Amazon
Advertise on LDP Amazon and Facebook page

Michael Gallon
***Other services available upon request. Additional charges may apply

Lock Down Publications
P.O. Box 944
Stockbridge, GA 30281-9998
Phone # 470 303-9761

Submission Guideline

Submit the first three chapters of your completed manuscript to ldpsubmissions@gmail.com, subject line: Your book's title. The manuscript must be in a .doc file and sent as an attachment. Document should be in Times New Roman, double spaced and in size 12 font. Also, provide your synopsis and full contact information. If sending multiple submissions, they must each be in a separate email.

Have a story but no way to send it electronically? You can still submit to LDP/Ca$h Presents. Send in the first three chapters, written or typed, of your completed manuscript to:

LDP: Submissions Dept
Po Box 944
Stockbridge, Ga 30281

DO NOT send original manuscript. Must be a duplicate.

Provide your synopsis and a cover letter containing your full contact information.

Thanks for considering LDP and Ca$h Presents.

NEW RELEASES

GORILLAZ IN THE TRENCHES 2 by SAYNOMORE

BLOOD OF A GOON by ROMELL TUKES

THE COCAINE PRINCESS 8 by KING RIO

THE MURDER QUEENS 3 by MICHAEL GALLON

Coming Soon from Lock Down Publications/Ca$h Presents

BLOOD OF A BOSS **VI**

SHADOWS OF THE GAME II

TRAP BASTARD II

By **Askari**

LOYAL TO THE GAME **IV**

By **T.J. & Jelissa**

TRUE SAVAGE **VIII**

MIDNIGHT CARTEL IV

DOPE BOY MAGIC IV

CITY OF KINGZ III

NIGHTMARE ON SILENT AVE II

THE PLUG OF LIL MEXICO II

CLASSIC CITY II

By **Chris Green**

BLAST FOR ME **III**

A SAVAGE DOPEBOY III

CUTTHROAT MAFIA III

DUFFLE BAG CARTEL VII

HEARTLESS GOON VI

By **Ghost**

A HUSTLER'S DECEIT III

KILL ZONE II

BAE BELONGS TO ME III

TIL DEATH II

By **Aryanna**

KING OF THE TRAP III

By **T.J. Edwards**

GORILLAZ IN THE BAY V

Michael Gallon

3X KRAZY III

STRAIGHT BEAST MODE III

De'Kari

KINGPIN KILLAZ IV

STREET KINGS III

PAID IN BLOOD III

CARTEL KILLAZ IV

DOPE GODS III

Hood Rich

SINS OF A HUSTLA II

ASAD

YAYO V

Bred In The Game 2

S. Allen

THE STREETS WILL TALK II

By Yolanda Moore

SON OF A DOPE FIEND III

HEAVEN GOT A GHETTO III

SKI MASK MONEY III

By Renta

LOYALTY AIN'T PROMISED III

By Keith Williams

I'M NOTHING WITHOUT HIS LOVE II

SINS OF A THUG II

TO THE THUG I LOVED BEFORE II

IN A HUSTLER I TRUST II

By Monet Dragun

QUIET MONEY IV

EXTENDED CLIP III

The Murder Queens 3
THUG LIFE IV

By **Trai'Quan**

THE STREETS MADE ME IV

By **Larry D. Wright**

IF YOU CROSS ME ONCE III

ANGEL V

By **Anthony Fields**

THE STREETS WILL NEVER CLOSE IV

By **K'ajji**

HARD AND RUTHLESS III

KILLA KOUNTY IV

By **Khufu**

MONEY GAME III

By **Smoove Dolla**

JACK BOYS VS DOPE BOYS IV

A GANGSTA'S QUR'AN V

COKE GIRLZ II

COKE BOYS II

LIFE OF A SAVAGE V

CHI'RAQ GANGSTAS V

SOSA GANG III

BRONX SAVAGES II

BODYMORE KINGPINS II

BLOOD OF A GOON II

By **Romell Tukes**

MURDA WAS THE CASE III

Elijah R. Freeman

AN UNFORESEEN LOVE IV

BABY, I'M WINTERTIME COLD III

Michael Gallon
By **Meesha**

QUEEN OF THE ZOO III

By **Black Migo**

CONFESSIONS OF A JACKBOY III

By **Nicholas Lock**

KING KILLA II

By **Vincent "Vitto" Holloway**

BETRAYAL OF A THUG III

By **Fre$h**

THE BIRTH OF A GANGSTER III

By **Delmont Player**

TREAL LOVE II

By **Le'Monica Jackson**

FOR THE LOVE OF BLOOD III

By **Jamel Mitchell**

RAN OFF ON DA PLUG II

By **Paper Boi Rari**

HOOD CONSIGLIERE III

By **Keese**

PRETTY GIRLS DO NASTY THINGS II

By **Nicole Goosby**

LOVE IN THE TRENCHES II

By **Corey Robinson**

IT'S JUST ME AND YOU II

By **Ah'Million**

FOREVER GANGSTA III

By **Adrian Dulan**

GORILLAZ IN THE TRENCHES III

The Murder Queens 3
By SayNoMore
THE COCAINE PRINCESS IX
By King Rio
CRIME BOSS II
Playa Ray
LOYALTY IS EVERYTHING III
Molotti
HERE TODAY GONE TOMORROW II
By Fly Rock
REAL G'S MOVE IN SILENCE II
By Von Diesel
GRIMEY WAYS IV
By Ray Vinci

<u>**Available Now**</u>

RESTRAINING ORDER **I & II**
By **CA$H & Coffee**
LOVE KNOWS NO BOUNDARIES **I II & III**
By **Coffee**
RAISED AS A GOON I, II, III & IV
BRED BY THE SLUMS I, II, III
BLAST FOR ME I & II
ROTTEN TO THE CORE I II III
A BRONX TALE I, II, III

Michael Gallon

DUFFLE BAG CARTEL I II III IV V VI

HEARTLESS GOON I II III IV V

A SAVAGE DOPEBOY I II

DRUG LORDS I II III

CUTTHROAT MAFIA I II

KING OF THE TRENCHES

By **Ghost**

LAY IT DOWN **I & II**

LAST OF A DYING BREED I II

BLOOD STAINS OF A SHOTTA I & II III

By **Jamaica**

LOYAL TO THE GAME I II III

LIFE OF SIN I, II III

By **TJ & Jelissa**

BLOODY COMMAS I & II

SKI MASK CARTEL I II & III

KING OF NEW YORK I II,III IV V

RISE TO POWER I II III

COKE KINGS I II III IV V

BORN HEARTLESS I II III IV

KING OF THE TRAP I II

By **T.J. Edwards**

IF LOVING HIM IS WRONG…I & II

LOVE ME EVEN WHEN IT HURTS I II III

By **Jelissa**

WHEN THE STREETS CLAP BACK I & II III

THE HEART OF A SAVAGE I II III IV

MONEY MAFIA I II

LOYAL TO THE SOIL I II III

The Murder Queens 3
By **Jibril Williams**
A DISTINGUISHED THUG STOLE MY HEART I II & III
LOVE SHOULDN'T HURT I II III IV
RENEGADE BOYS I II III IV
PAID IN KARMA I II III
SAVAGE STORMS I II III
AN UNFORESEEN LOVE I II III
BABY, I'M WINTERTIME COLD I II
By **Meesha**
A GANGSTER'S CODE I &, II III
A GANGSTER'S SYN I II III
THE SAVAGE LIFE I II III
CHAINED TO THE STREETS I II III
BLOOD ON THE MONEY I II III
A GANGSTA'S PAIN I II III
By J-Blunt
PUSH IT TO THE LIMIT
By **Bre' Hayes**
BLOOD OF A BOSS **I, II, III, IV, V**
SHADOWS OF THE GAME
TRAP BASTARD
By **Askari**
THE STREETS BLEED MURDER **I, II & III**
THE HEART OF A GANGSTA I II& III
By **Jerry Jackson**
CUM FOR ME I II III IV V VI VII VIII
An **LDP Erotica Collaboration**
BRIDE OF A HUSTLA **I II & II**
THE FETTI GIRLS **I, II& III**

Michael Gallon
CORRUPTED BY A GANGSTA I, II III, IV

BLINDED BY HIS LOVE

THE PRICE YOU PAY FOR LOVE I, II ,III

DOPE GIRL MAGIC I II III

By **Destiny Skai**

WHEN A GOOD GIRL GOES BAD

By **Adrienne**

THE COST OF LOYALTY I II III

By Kweli

A GANGSTER'S REVENGE **I II III & IV**

THE BOSS MAN'S DAUGHTERS I II III IV V

A SAVAGE LOVE **I & II**

BAE BELONGS TO ME I II

A HUSTLER'S DECEIT I, II, III

WHAT BAD BITCHES DO I, II, III

SOUL OF A MONSTER I II III

KILL ZONE

A DOPE BOY'S QUEEN I II III

TIL DEATH

By **Aryanna**

A KINGPIN'S AMBITON

A KINGPIN'S AMBITION **II**

I MURDER FOR THE DOUGH

By **Ambitious**

TRUE SAVAGE I II III IV V VI VII

DOPE BOY MAGIC I, II, III

MIDNIGHT CARTEL I II III

CITY OF KINGZ I II

NIGHTMARE ON SILENT AVE

THE PLUG OF LIL MEXICO II

CLASSIC CITY

By **Chris Green**

A DOPEBOY'S PRAYER

By **Eddie "Wolf" Lee**

THE KING CARTEL **I, II & III**

By **Frank Gresham**

THESE NIGGAS AIN'T LOYAL **I, II & III**

By **Nikki Tee**

GANGSTA SHYT **I II &III**

By **CATO**

THE ULTIMATE BETRAYAL

By **Phoenix**

BOSS'N UP **I , II & III**

By **Royal Nicole**

I LOVE YOU TO DEATH

By **Destiny J**

I RIDE FOR MY HITTA

I STILL RIDE FOR MY HITTA

By **Misty Holt**

LOVE & CHASIN' PAPER

By **Qay Crockett**

TO DIE IN VAIN

SINS OF A HUSTLA

By **ASAD**

BROOKLYN HUSTLAZ

By **Boogsy Morina**

BROOKLYN ON LOCK I & II

By **Sonovia**

Michael Gallon

GANGSTA CITY

By **Teddy Duke**

A DRUG KING AND HIS DIAMOND I & II III

A DOPEMAN'S RICHES

HER MAN, MINE'S TOO I, II

CASH MONEY HO'S

THE WIFEY I USED TO BE I II

PRETTY GIRLS DO NASTY THINGS

By **Nicole Goosby**

TRAPHOUSE KING **I II & III**

KINGPIN KILLAZ I II III

STREET KINGS I II

PAID IN BLOOD **I II**

CARTEL KILLAZ I II III

DOPE GODS I II

By **Hood Rich**

LIPSTICK KILLAH **I, II, III**

CRIME OF PASSION I II & III

FRIEND OR FOE I II III

By **Mimi**

STEADY MOBBN' **I, II, III**

THE STREETS STAINED MY SOUL I II III

By **Marcellus Allen**

WHO SHOT YA **I, II, III**

SON OF A DOPE FIEND I II

HEAVEN GOT A GHETTO I II

SKI MASK MONEY I II

Renta

GORILLAZ IN THE BAY **I II III IV**

The Murder Queens 3
TEARS OF A GANGSTA I II
3X KRAZY I II
STRAIGHT BEAST MODE I II

DE'KARI
TRIGGADALE I II III
MURDAROBER WAS THE CASE I II

Elijah R. Freeman
GOD BLESS THE TRAPPERS I, II, III
THESE SCANDALOUS STREETS I, II, III
FEAR MY GANGSTA I, II, III IV, V
THESE STREETS DON'T LOVE NOBODY I, II
BURY ME A G I, II, III, IV, V
A GANGSTA'S EMPIRE I, II, III, IV
THE DOPEMAN'S BODYGAURD I II
THE REALEST KILLAZ I II III
THE LAST OF THE OGS I II III

Tranay Adams
THE STREETS ARE CALLING

Duquie Wilson
MARRIED TO A BOSS I II III

By Destiny Skai & Chris Green
KINGZ OF THE GAME I II III IV V VI VII
CRIME BOSS

Playa Ray
SLAUGHTER GANG I II III
RUTHLESS HEART I II III

By Willie Slaughter
FUK SHYT

By Blakk Diamond

Michael Gallon
DON'T F#CK WITH MY HEART I II
By Linnea
ADDICTED TO THE DRAMA I II III
IN THE ARM OF HIS BOSS II
By Jamila
YAYO I II III IV
A SHOOTER'S AMBITION I II
BRED IN THE GAME
By S. Allen
TRAP GOD I II III
RICH $AVAGE I II III
MONEY IN THE GRAVE I II III
By Martell Troublesome Bolden
FOREVER GANGSTA I II
GLOCKS ON SATIN SHEETS I II
By Adrian Dulan
TOE TAGZ I II III IV
LEVELS TO THIS SHYT I II
IT'S JUST ME AND YOU
By Ah'Million
KINGPIN DREAMS I II III
RAN OFF ON DA PLUG
By Paper Boi Rari
CONFESSIONS OF A GANGSTA I II III IV
CONFESSIONS OF A JACKBOY I II
By Nicholas Lock
I'M NOTHING WITHOUT HIS LOVE
SINS OF A THUG
TO THE THUG I LOVED BEFORE

154

The Murder Queens 3

A GANGSTA SAVED XMAS

IN A HUSTLER I TRUST

By Monet Dragun

CAUGHT UP IN THE LIFE I II III

THE STREETS NEVER LET GO I II III

By Robert Baptiste

NEW TO THE GAME I II III

MONEY, MURDER & MEMORIES I II III

By Malik D. Rice

LIFE OF A SAVAGE I II III IV

A GANGSTA'S QUR'AN I II III IV

MURDA SEASON I II III

GANGLAND CARTEL I II III

CHI'RAQ GANGSTAS I II III IV

KILLERS ON ELM STREET I II III

JACK BOYZ N DA BRONX I II III

A DOPEBOY'S DREAM I II III

JACK BOYS VS DOPE BOYS I II III

COKE GIRLZ

COKE BOYS

SOSA GANG I II

BRONX SAVAGES

BODYMORE KINGPINS

BLOOD OF A GOON

By Romell Tukes

LOYALTY AIN'T PROMISED I II

By Keith Williams

QUIET MONEY I II III

THUG LIFE I II III

Michael Gallon
EXTENDED CLIP I II
A GANGSTA'S PARADISE
By **Trai'Quan**
THE STREETS MADE ME I II III
By **Larry D. Wright**
THE ULTIMATE SACRIFICE I, II, III, IV, V, VI
KHADIFI
IF YOU CROSS ME ONCE I II
ANGEL I II III IV
IN THE BLINK OF AN EYE
By **Anthony Fields**
THE LIFE OF A HOOD STAR
By **Ca$h & Rashia Wilson**
THE STREETS WILL NEVER CLOSE I II III
By **K'ajji**
CREAM I II III
THE STREETS WILL TALK
By **Yolanda Moore**
NIGHTMARES OF A HUSTLA I II III
By **King Dream**
CONCRETE KILLA I II III
VICIOUS LOYALTY I II III
By **Kingpen**
HARD AND RUTHLESS I II
MOB TOWN 251
THE BILLIONAIRE BENTLEYS I II III
REAL G'S MOVE IN SILENCE
By **Von Diesel**
GHOST MOB

The Murder Queens 3
Stilloan Robinson
MOB TIES I II III IV V VI
SOUL OF A HUSTLER, HEART OF A KILLER I II
GORILLAZ IN THE TRENCHES I II
By SayNoMore
BODYMORE MURDERLAND I II III
THE BIRTH OF A GANGSTER I II
By Delmont Player
FOR THE LOVE OF A BOSS
By C. D. Blue
MOBBED UP I II III IV
THE BRICK MAN I II III IV V
THE COCAINE PRINCESS I II III IV V VI VII VIII
By King Rio
KILLA KOUNTY I II III IV
By Khufu
MONEY GAME I II
By Smoove Dolla
A GANGSTA'S KARMA I II III
By FLAME
KING OF THE TRENCHES I II III
by **GHOST & TRANAY ADAMS**
QUEEN OF THE ZOO I II
By **Black Migo**
GRIMEY WAYS I II III
By Ray Vinci
XMAS WITH AN ATL SHOOTER
By Ca$h & Destiny Skai
KING KILLA

Michael Gallon
By Vincent "Vitto" Holloway

BETRAYAL OF A THUG I II

By Fre$h

THE MURDER QUEENS I II III

By Michael Gallon

TREAL LOVE

By Le'Monica Jackson

FOR THE LOVE OF BLOOD I II

By Jamel Mitchell

HOOD CONSIGLIERE I II

By Keese

PROTÉGÉ OF A LEGEND I II III

LOVE IN THE TRENCHES

By Corey Robinson

BORN IN THE GRAVE I II III

By Self Made Tay

MOAN IN MY MOUTH

By XTASY

TORN BETWEEN A GANGSTER AND A GENTLEMAN

By J-BLUNT & Miss Kim

LOYALTY IS EVERYTHING I II

Molotti

HERE TODAY GONE TOMORROW

By Fly Rock

PILLOW PRINCESS

By S. Hawkins

NAÏVE TO THE STREETS

WOMEN LIE MEN LIE I II III

GIRLS FALL LIKE DOMINOS

158

The Murder Queens 3
STACK BEFORE YOU SPURLGE

By A. Roy Milligan

BOOKS BY LDP'S CEO, CA$H

TRUST IN NO MAN

TRUST IN NO MAN 2

TRUST IN NO MAN 3

BONDED BY BLOOD

SHORTY GOT A THUG

THUGS CRY

THUGS CRY 2

THUGS CRY 3

TRUST NO BITCH

TRUST NO BITCH 2

TRUST NO BITCH 3

TIL MY CASKET DROPS

RESTRAINING ORDER

RESTRAINING ORDER 2

IN LOVE WITH A CONVICT

LIFE OF A HOOD STAR

XMAS WITH AN ATL SHOOTER

CPSIA information can be obtained
at www.ICGtesting.com
Printed in the USA
LVHW010807170523
747217LV00008B/600